That day, he looked up toward her house, squinted, as if he truly saw her, searched for something hidden behind her eyes. Just her nerves, she told herself, he couldn't have seen her eyes. Perhaps, however, the sun had reflected off the binoculars. She stepped to the side of the window, pressed her back against the wall, suddenly hot with shame. Not for watching him, but for the phone calls she made to the Border Patrol, about him, his friends, cars they drove, what they looked like. Maybe, she thought that day, it is time to stop. She never imagined it would lead to this.

—FROM "EVEN IN HEAVEN"

'yrical and quietly powerful stories bring
ets of the town of Mesquite.

Heaven" a now prosperous woman who
the country illegally decades before
e border with binoculars and reports unlaw-
s—but what she really sees is a new way of
er past. In another story, a woman about
vith her lover is confronted by her husband,
because she has moved a certain picture on
In a third, two young brothers infatuated
same self-possessed girl adopt different atti-
sweet and shocking results.

worlds created by Gabriel García Márquez
a Esquivel, Mesquite is a special, unforget-
ee. Its people have an indomitable passion
bility to find joy even when chasing shadows.

Chasing Shadows

Chasing Shadows

Stories   Lucrecia Guerrero

CHRONICLE BOOKS
SAN FRANCISCO

I would like to thank the Ohio Arts Council and the Montgomery County Arts and Cultural District for their support.

Earlier versions of some of the stories in this collection originally appeared in the following publications: "The Girdle" in the *Dayton Daily News;* "Blanca Rosa" in *El Locofoco;* and "Gloves of Her Own" in *ByLine*.

Library of Congress Cataloging-in-Publication Data:

Guerrero, Lucrecia.
    Chasing shadows : stories / Lucrecia Guerrero.
    p.   cm.
    Contents: Even in heaven—The curse—The girdle—Memories in white—Blanca Rosa—Gloves of her own—Butterfly—Hotel Arco Iris—Love and happiness—Cloud-shadow—Return of the spirit.
ISBN 0-8118-2794-1 (pbk.)
1. Mexican-American Border Region—Social life and customs—Fiction.
2. Mexican-Americans—Mexican-American Border Region—Fiction. I. Title.

PS3557.U342 C47 2000
8138.54—dc21   99-055166
                                                      CIP

Printed in the United States.

Designed by Jeremy Stout
Typesetting by Star Type, Berkeley
Cover background photographs by Masako Takahashi

DISTRIBUTED IN CANADA BY RAINCOAST BOOKS
8680 CAMBIE STREET
VANCOUVER, BRITISH COLUMBIA V6P 6M9

10 9 8 7 6 5 4 3 2 1

CHRONICLE BOOKS
85 SECOND STREET
SAN FRANCISCO, CALIFORNIA 94105

WWW.CHRONICLEBOOKS.COM

To the memory of my sister,
Clydia Alejandra Guerrero.

Contents

even in heaven

A YELPING BARK SOUNDS FROM BELOW, and Cookie McDonald looks away from the pot of apples precariously balanced on her lap. Her gaze travels beyond her backyard—fenced in to keep out stray dogs—down the decline dotted with sagebrush and nopal cactus, stops at the bottom of the hill, Frontera Street. A large yellow dog lies in the dirt, lifts its head, howls. Cookie's eyes shift toward the dead end of Frontera: An apartment building of crumbling brick sits in the U.S. but faces the tall chain-link fence that center-cuts the length of the street, separates Mesquite from Mexico. If only she had her binoculars with her.

But her daughter, Nancy, is in the house. Better she doesn't find out about them, Cookie thinks. Anyway, she has been considering not informing anymore, returning the binoculars to Peter.

She turns back to her apples, hums a lullaby from her childhood, and gently swings in the glider her husband placed under the shade of a scrubby walnut tree. Shafts of sunlight cut through the canopy of leaves, warm the exposed tops of her feet. She tucks her legs under the glider's shadow. In Ohio, after she married Bill and escaped the tomato fields, it was easy to maintain her winter-skin shade of sallow tan (lightened with a generous layer of ivory Angel

Face powder). Now they live in Arizona. The western sun, harsh as truth itself, normally forces her inside, out of the light that could turn her an Aztec brown. But today Nancy's arguments about that man disturb the shadowed sanctuary of their home.

Cookie peels an apple, holds the scalloped length of skin between her thumb and index finger, admires its unbroken, downward spiral, drops it into a plastic bag. Her eyes slide to a basket half-full of Granny Smiths. Will she need more for her celebration dinner tonight? Twenty years. Can it be that long since she left Mexico and her position as maid in Doña Inez's house?

She wishes she could forget the past, ignore all that happened before she married, another self shed somewhere along the way. Although lately, with the marking of her anniversary in this country, memories long since buried, gauze-faint tendrils, creep up, crawl through her dreams.

Odors waft up to Edwards Street from Frontera: chiles roasting, beans frying in lard, tortillas warming on the comal. Her eyes follow the scent, memories of the child she used to be. Below, a screen door swings open, a tall man steps out, Joaquín de la Torre. The Chicano, the troublemaker with eyes like smoking mirrors.

"Mother," Nancy calls out from behind her. Watching Cookie from the kitchen window? "Why are you wearing that long-sleeved blouse when it's almost a hundred degrees outside? This isn't Ohio, you know. Everybody's got a tan down here, it's okay to be dark like you."

Cookie swallows. Nancy knows how sensitive she is about her complexion. "You say these things because you are angry, but I don't change my mind. That Chicano is not coming to dinner," Cookie says. "All the people know he is no good. Already because of him you want to hurt your own mother with your words. I don't want no more talk about him." She selects another apple from the basket.

Their kitchen door squeaks. Without looking up, Cookie pats the space next to her on the glider. When Nancy sits down, the swing lowers and tilts slightly with her weight.

"I wasn't trying to hurt your feelings, Mom." When Cookie doesn't respond, Nancy's voice hardens. "Pies?" she says and looks at the deep pot filled with water and apples on Cookie's lap. "Does it have to be apple? They never taste right the way you make them. Anyway, if they're for Dad's benefit, well, this is Friday, remember?"

Cookie understands: Friday, Bill's night to close the Montezuma Cocktail Lounge, stumble past their bedroom when he finally comes home, throw himself on the daybed in the guest room. No doubt he stares at the closet door there, fantasizes about the slide trombone stored in a locked black case, his life's dream sacrificed for a forced marriage. But this morning, didn't she remind him that today is special? So, yes, she remembers what day it is, but she will ignore Nancy's remark. Sometimes it is better to pretend you cannot understand. Why make arguments?

"Well, at least can't we make something sort of south-western?" Nancy says.

"This is a special meal." The words sound dry, dead wood. Cookie takes a deep breath, brightens her tone. "Today I make an all-American dinner: pan-fried chicken, mashed potatoes and gravy, corn on the cob with sweet butter. And apple pie."

"Southwestern's not American?" Nancy says. "It's a lot like Mexican food. You can cook that, can't you? You're Mexican."

"I have twenty years in this country." Cookie slaps the last word down, exclamation point. She has worked so hard all these years to turn her now fifteen-year-old daughter into an all-American girl, never discusses her own life in Mexico. Nancy has no reason to feel foreign. Why this sudden interest in a culture that has nothing to do with her?

"I know, I know," Nancy says, pushes on the dusty ground with the toe of her shoe, jerks the swing forward, then suddenly backward.

Cookie grabs at the pot. The water sloshes up the stainless-steel wall but not over the rim. She looks sharply at Nancy, but Nancy turns her head, a profile so innocent, so calm, Cookie chooses to believe the near upset was accidental. Why look for problems? She follows Nancy's gaze although she knows it leads back to him.

Joaquín stands by the cab of his pickup, parked in the dirt lot of the apartments. The first time Cookie saw him, he stood in much the same place. Only then, he rubbed the dust from his truck with a cloth, almost brought a shine to the time-scarred surface. He wore no shirt, his chest bare, the skin smooth and hairless like his ancestors. Although her arms ached holding up the binoculars, she watched for over ten minutes, fascinated with the ripple of each muscle beneath his brown skin. *Her father, Papi, swinging a machete, whirr-slice, whirr-slice, ancient song humming through the mountain air. So long ago.* It was Joaquín's hands that held her captive: large and strong like a worker's, but unexpectedly well-shaped, the fingers long and tapered. Aristocratic? She could almost feel their touch, fingertips pressing at the far-off drumbeat of her pulse, some memory awakening deep inside her.

That day, he looked up toward her house, squinted, as if he truly saw her, searched for something hidden behind her eyes. Just her nerves, she told herself, he couldn't have seen her eyes. Perhaps, however, the sun had reflected off the binoculars. She stepped to the side of the window, pressed her back against the wall, suddenly hot with shame. Not for watching him, but for the phone calls she made to the Border Patrol, about him, his friends, cars they drove, what they looked like. Maybe, she thought that day, it is time to stop. She never imagined it would lead to this.

She reaches out, touches Nancy's forearm. "No," she says, "that one is not for you. Too old."

Nancy's arm stiffens and she pulls it in toward herself. "He's only nineteen, Mom. See what I mean? You don't know a thing about him. Meet him, see how neat he is. He likes to talk about history, stuff about Mexico and Indians— the indigenous people, that is—and politics, all kinds of things. The other day—I just overheard him talking— anyway, he was telling a story about an Indian named La Malinche."

Cookie tightens her grips on the pot, thinks of the binoculars pushed far back on a high shelf where Nancy will not find them. "Everybody knows about La Malinche," Cookie says. "You don't have to be smart for that. He is just a Chicano, how can he understand Mexican history? Life?"

Nancy studies her, curious. "It's just so weird, you never want to talk about Mexico. What's the big deal?" Nancy says.

"The past is gone, not important for nothing. To survive it is necessary to concentrate on now."

"Tell that to my history teacher," Nancy says. She rushes on, determined to finish. "Anyway, this is a real neat story. Seems this Indian, Malinche, went with Cortez, you know, the Spanish explorer guy, helped him against her own people, or something like that."

Cookie waves her hand, bats at the words. "An old story."

"Lots of people say she was a traitor, but Joaquín says we got to consider her situation. I don't see how anybody can excuse her, but that just goes to show you what kind of a guy he is. So then, Malinche and Cortez had babies, which is what you call the Mestizo people. Like us. Cool, huh?"

"What like us? Ridiculous talk from an ignorant cotton-picker. Maybe those people make problems, do what they are not supposed to do, don't want to accept their destiny. He will fill your head with illusions." She did not realize how ragged her breathing had become until she saw Nancy's expression.

"I don't get it, what's the big deal?" Nancy says, but doesn't wait for an explanation. "You just don't like him because he's poor. Well, he's going to go to college one of these days, he's got plans."

Cookie shakes her head from side to side. "Forget him. He is nothing—a dreamer. I ask about him to the neighbors. Mrs. Peterson say he is involved with students from the university—but don't think he is one of them—and something with the migrant workers, telling them who knows what. No," she says, "I tell you, this boy make problems, that is what Mrs. Peterson say."

"It's *says,* Mom. Mrs. Peterson *says.*"

Cookie's face stings, but she only looks down at her hands, presses her lips together in silence. She is never certain about discipline. Maybe Nancy's behavior is okay for Americans. After all these years, she is still unsure. She watches television and tries to copy the American TV mothers—Mrs. Cleaver and Mrs. Anderson, models of what the perfect American woman should be. She hears their words but does not feel them. When the program ends after thirty minutes, too many questions remain un-answered.

And the fathers on those programs, they talk with the mother, help with decisions involving the children. Not Bill.

"Home and hearth's your department, kiddo," he says. "You're the one that got yourself pregnant and reeled in a husband and citizenship. Nobody can say you don't know how to pick a sucker." He laughs, gives her a look she knows too well, reminds her that to fulfill his obligations he took a sensible job with an insurance company, forgot his plans to travel with the Dukes of Dreamland Dance Band.

Cookie presses index finger and thumb to the bridge of her nose. Her headache is spreading, pricks of pain behind her eyes.

"I got to go," Nancy says and jumps up.

"Where?" Cookie says, looks down the hill. Joaquín and his truck are gone. She grabs and holds on to the tail of Nancy's shirt, an old one of Bill's she wears over jeans rolled up to her knees.

Nancy tugs at her shirt until Cookie releases it. "Got to see some friends at the library."

"Stay in the shade or you will ruin your color," Cookie says, but the words bounce off Nancy's back as she disappears around the corner of the house. Through half-closed eyes she watches the yellow dog slowly making its way up the slope to her house, some bit of garbage from the apartments below clamped in its jaws. It stops halfway, lies down, massive head on paws, chews its loot, returns her gaze until she is forced to turn away.

Cookie presses her eyes shut, pushes away the image of the dog, wills her mind to close it out. She pictures her daughter, wishes she could tell Nancy a story that would help her understand why she should be grateful for her complexion—a story that would explain Cookie's concern with color. But even the memory humiliates her.

Well, enough of that, she thinks. What was it her mistress, Doña Inez, from those long-ago days, used to say: Qué se puede hacer? What can be done?

Careful not to knock the brim of her sun hat, Cookie leans back, surveys their new yard. Bill's asthma brought them here; she hadn't wanted to leave Ohio, travel to Arizona and this city that splits into two countries. But she accepted the inevitable and was determined to adapt, just as she always has. She even hoped the move would bring her and her family closer together. Instead, Nancy insists on pretending she is one of these Chicanos. It's only a game for her; she doesn't see that it could close doors to her.

And the strange surroundings haven't kept Bill home nights. No, he has found a new bar, new friends. One night, he brought home Peter.

While standing at the kitchen window, Peter looked down the hill, said, "We're being overrun by illegals, they're coming in left and right. I tell you, we got our work cut out for us. Word is, somebody down there's not helping the situation. Sure would be nice if a good citizen would keep an eye on things, let us know who's coming and going, license plates, stuff like that, maybe give us a call down to the Border Patrol."

He went out to his car, came back with a small leather case. "It's not like I don't understand people wanting to get ahead. Why, my own grandmother came over here from County Cork, Ireland, but it's got to stop someplace, for Chrissakes." He held out the glasses to her. "Now, don't feel obligated. But I tell you what, it's people like you who can do the most good." He placed one hand on her shoulder. "It'd be a real nice gesture, a chance to show where your heart is. Know what I mean?"

She hesitated before taking the binoculars. "Nobody would suspect you," Peter said and laughed.

After he left, Bill told her she shouldn't feel obligated. "Let them do their own dirty work," he said. But she said she would prove her loyalty once and for all. Fingers at her temples now, steady circles. Peter is correct, one cannot be concerned with the world's problems. Life hasn't been easy for her, after all, but look at her. A peasant and housemaid in her native Mexico, here she is a homeowner and considered a member of the middle class. Doesn't she have a right to protect her position?

She sighs. If only her former mistress, Doña Inez, and the rest of the Montalba family could see her. The Montalbas with their *good blood* and so certain of God's preference. The Montalbas, whose memory she has pushed aside for so long, but who now creep back into her consciousness as surely as the sunlight filters through her closed eyelids.

She recalls another one of Doña Inez's statements: "Even in heaven," she would say, "the angels are not equal. Qué se puede hacer?" Doña Inez would shrug her shoulders and glance apologetically toward her maid.

Cookie opens her eyes, brushes away a green fly that buzzes around her head. But with the constant droning and the lulling heat, her lids soon droop again, and in spite of herself, her thoughts drift back to dinner celebrations long ago.

Every year Cuca, as she was called then, prepared the mole poblano for her mistress's Saint's Day. On that day, all of Doña Inez's children, along with their heirs, visited in the decaying neighborhood where they had been reared.

Keeping one ear alert for the tinkle of the silver dinner bell, Cuca stirred the chocolate-rich sauce with a wooden spoon, careful to avoid the bubbles that broke on the surface. For within each miniature globe, she saw the distant face of Alexandro Montalba Contreras, both grandson and second cousin to Doña Inez. And Cuca watched her own hands (the thick, broad fingernails, now narrow and delicate, and the strong, short fingers, now as long and aristocratic as his) skim over his face, fingertips caressing each innately arrogant feature. Then the bubble would burst and roll back under into the hot liquid, taking with it a piece of her heart.

Alexandro couldn't be for her, and not just because she was poor and they, wealthy. Even in heaven, the angels are not equal. Throughout the generations, the Montalbas had guarded against what they called dañando la sangre, damaging the blood; even after they had lost so much of their land and power during the agrarian revolution—which Doña Inez still remembered with great sorrow. In their family, they claimed, there were only Christian Europeans who could trace their roots back to the Spanish aristocracy.

Sometimes the blood wasn't so pure, but Cuca knew better than to mention this. She looked back over her shoulder at the child Graciela, who sat at the kitchen table, her head bent over the plate of rice that she scooped up with pieces of tortilla. "Stop eating like an Indian," Cuca chided and started to smack the girl's hand with the spoon. But why? When would her aunt Inez see her eat? For as the illegitimate daughter of one of the Montalba men, Graciela had only been taken in because she had no one else to care for her.

On Graciela's first day there, Doña Inez had informed her that she would be provided for, but she must assist Cuca in her housework. And although she could call Doña Inez aunt, it was clear that the privileges of blood stopped there. Graciela took all her meals in the kitchen with Cuca even when there was no company. Sometimes Cuca felt sympathy for the girl, but more often, she had only to look at Graciela and a sudden anger would surge up like hot vomit in her throat. At least Graciela, with her tiny claims of *good blood,* might have some chance to break out of this bitter circle, but what future did Cuca have?

She had been brought into the Montalba household when she was no older than Graciela. There had never been any doubt about Cuca's position—neither of her parents were one of God's preferred angels. No, she was the daughter of poor peasants. Her father, who had left his family when Cuca was just a baby, became a memory as elusive as a wisp of mountain mist from her village. He had gone to the north in search of work; he would send home money, he said. But she and her mother never heard from him again, never knew his fate. When Cuca's mother died of tuberculosis a few years later, Cuca left to make her own way in Mexico City. She had been thankful for Doña Inez then.

Cuca turned back to the stove, an antiquity from the Spanish Colonial period that Doña Inez refused to relinquish, and fanned the coals with a straw fan. Maybe loving Alexandro wasn't so silly. After all, he was different from the others. Didn't he always make pretty speeches about the poor, and didn't he anger his grandmother when he defended the revolution that had robbed her of her birthright? And last year, at the reunion, hadn't he insisted that Cuca use the familiar *tu* instead of the formal *usted* with him, as if they were equals? Maybe the angels in heaven were equal (although, of course, she never accepted Alexandro's offer, for she knew the scandal it would cause).

Still, Alexandro was a Montalba. Cuca listened to his relatives, their confident voices that penetrated the door leading to the dining room. "Please, Mother, won't you move in with one of us?" their voices chorused. It was the same conversation they had every year.

But Cuca knew Doña Inez would never leave her home, so full of ancestral ghosts hovering, waiting. They were tenacious spirits that laughed softly as they wrapped around Cuca when, on her hands and knees, she attempted to scrub them away from the shadowy corners of the rooms.

The delicate bell, with the words Recuerdo de Mexico, remembrance of Mexico, inscribed on its inner side, sounded and Cuca stiffened. When she entered the dining room, her face wore no expression other than a half smile, slight enough to make her face pleasant, yet not wide enough to suggest familiarity.

"Are you planning to bring out the next dish, or are you on vacation?" said Doña Inez's middle-aged daughter Carmina, who still behaved like a spoiled child.

Cuca, in her shame at being scolded in front of Alexandro, tried to concentrate on a spot on the wall, over and beyond his head. She needn't have. He focused his attention on a visiting cousin who sat to his right. Alexandro's eyes clouded with adoration as he gazed at the Montalba face, a female version of his own. For a moment, Cuca forgot herself and stared openly at them. She stared so hard, the borders of the cousins' faces blurred, became one.

How could she have been such a fool as to think that Alexandro ever saw her, Refugio Alvarez, as a flesh-and-blood woman? She was no more real to him than his fancy words and ideas. In that moment, she hated Alexandro, cursed all the nights she had drifted off to sleep with his image in her heart. He was nothing more than a dreamer. What did he know of life beyond his books, his precious family? There was no place for her in his plans; they would not marry and live happily ever after as she had hoped. She knew then that it was up to her to pave her own road.

Back in the kitchen, Cuca ladled turkey and sauce onto the plates and said to Graciela, "You, girl, wake up. They're finished with the rice. Go collect their plates. Now." When Graciela didn't answer, Cuca turned to see her still hunched over in her chair, daydreaming as usual. Cuca snapped her fingers. "Do you hear me, muchacha? And don't give me that insolent face of yours."

Graciela eased off the edge of the chair, but too slowly, it seemed to Cuca. She reached out, pinched the girl's smooth arm. The child opened her mouth, but Cuca covered it with her hand. She whispered, "Better not cry. They don't like problems when they're having a good time."

Cuca averted her eyes when she saw the red mark her pinch had left, but also (though she would never admit it, not even in the confessional) felt pleased when she thought of the bruise that would surely appear on that pale Montalba skin. With a damp corner of her apron, she dabbed at Graciela's tears. "Come on now, be a good girl. I know you don't like to serve them. Qué se puede hacer?"

But as Graciela shuffled away, Cuca made a decision. For years others had told her about the United States. One adventurer had even told her about a man from a rich and famous family who had married a servant. Yes, she would take the money she had saved up in a clay water jug and make the trip. The time had come.

That day she promised herself her children would never be anyone's servants. They would be among God's favorite angels, just like the Montalbas. With those thoughts, she made plans to join her friends in the tomato fields of Ohio.

Cookie stirs, swats at the fly that persists in flitting about her, but it darts away. She opens her eyes wide, as if she could force her memories out. Remembering only complicates her life, makes decisions more difficult. She encircles her arms around the pot, returns to the cool interior of her house. Inside, she leans against the doorsill, waits for her sun-blinded eyes to grow accustomed to the shadows before she takes the apples to the sink. She stares at them; rounded globes become lenses. Staring back at her.

Sometimes, when she observed Joaquín's apartment, she saw an older woman. His mother, no doubt. A woman like so many Cookie remembers from her youth. Good, strong. A woman who adores her child. What if something happens to Joaquín?

She sways, suddenly tired. Nancy is right about her pies; all these years and she still cannot get the recipe right. Forget the apple pies. Forget the binoculars?

She wipes her hands on her gingham apron and turns to the kitchen table, twists the dial of the radio until she finds KOMA, the station out of Oklahoma City. Nancy's favorite station, it plays the Top 40 over and over. For Cookie, music is somehow like a dream, something that reaches your inner being. Maybe it will reveal her daughter to her.

Outside, the dog barks. Cookie goes to the window. It has made its way to her fence, won't stop yapping, chipping away at her peace of mind as insistently as a memory that won't be forgotten. What does it want from her? Let it starve. She won't let it in her yard. She'll have Bill run barbed wire around the fence. Like the taller one at the border. Of course, she should have thought of it earlier. And she'll go to the garden store tomorrow, find a high hedge, something dense to grow along the perimeter. Someday it will grow so high she won't be able to see the street below. But until then, she will keep the binoculars.

the Curse

THE FLOORBOARD CREAKS BEHIND FLACO; he jumps
to the side, away from the box of cookies. *Whoosh*. An arm
slices through the air, only inches from where he was
standing. He turns. Their mother takes aim this time, swings
at Flaco's older brother, Riquis. Riquis ducks and her fist,
little bits of tortilla dough clinging to it, grazes his back,
glances off his shoulder, leaves powder-white traces of
flour on his striped T-shirt. Riquis drops the cookies. Then
in one motion, as smooth as El Santo in the comic books,
he crouches and darts out the kitchen door.

"Azufre," their mother yells, "you stink of sulfur, you
demonio, you're cursed."

Flaco runs out behind his brother, but when he shoots
a glance back over his shoulder, he sees it's safe for now:
Mami's hands are pressed to her face and she is crying.
Again. Flaco unfolds his arm—jackknifed behind his head
in a protective *V,* just in case. He knows that he and Riquis
should have stayed outside most of the day, not only because of Mami but also because their baby sister, Olga, has
been bawling almost nonstop. They only sneaked back in to
take some cookies. He managed to shove two into his jeans
pocket before she came up behind them, but Riquis was
caught in the act. And today Mami is not in a good mood.

Didn't he know that right from the start? He heard her banging things around in the kitchen, started early this morning with the coffeepot, which is already dented. Next thing she was gagging, vomiting in the scrub bucket she keeps under the sink; then she ran out the door—slammed it so hard the windows rattled—to go empty the bucket in the outside toilet. When she starts banging and slamming, it's mostly Riquis who has to watch out because he looks so much like Papi. Sometimes Flaco feels sorry for his brother, but at the same time, deep inside, he's glad that Riquis is there to get it because otherwise it might be him.

After he follows Riquis around the corner of their apartment building, Riquis stops and whirls to face him, throws out his chest like the fighting cocks. "What are you looking, pinche pendejo? Didn't you ever see no devil before? That's right, I'm a demonio. You heard what she said."

Flaco stares at the ground, says nothing. When Riquis's breathing slows down, Flaco pulls the cookies out of his pocket: soft wafers with a mound of coconut-sprinkled marshmallow, the kind their father always brings when he comes home late. The marshmallow has melted together, and he pulls them apart, gives one to Riquis. They stuff their mouths with the cookies.

"You're not the devil, man; I don't smell no sulfur." Flaco's words squish out around the marshmallow. "She's only saying that."

Riquis opens his mouth wide, sticks out his tongue, shows the chewed-up, saliva-mixed lump of cookie. After he shuts his mouth again and swallows, he says, "Eat shit, Mami's little baby." Riquis's eyes narrow, shift to the apartment to their left. Flaco follows his gaze. A small gray cat with a white star in the middle of its forehead lies curled up on the cracked concrete outside the screen door, returns their gaze through half-closed eyes—one blue and the other, slightly crossed, green.

"Oh, the devil's been around, all right," Riquis mumbles. "Who do you think put a curse on me?" His voice is low, like he doesn't want the cat to hear. "That's why Mami caught *me,* not you. And, anyway, don't you notice how things have been worse since she came here?" He jerks his head toward the apartment to their side.

"Who? The cat?" Flaco says, all the while studies its green eye, tries to cross one of his own eyes.

"Not the cat, pendejo—well, kind of the cat. But mostly it's the girl. What's her name?"

"Tonantzin," Flaco says, even though he's sure Riquis knows it better than he does. She is in Riquis's class in school and Riquis was the one who kept staring at her that first day she moved in with her father, a broken-down boxer. El Kid Salazar sits outside at night, when he's in town, holds a raw beefsteak over his black eye and talks about how he was outweighed or how the other guy hit below the belt or some other reason why he never wins. Sure, sure, Flaco always thinks when he hears these stories.

"Yeah, Toenail, that's her name," Riquis says. "I bet you anything you want she's been putting curses on people. Her and that damn gato of hers. Hell, I can smell the sulfur, like Mami says, but it's not me, man. It's like I said, things have been bad since *she* moved into the barrio."

"Pues . . ." Flaco grinds one heel into the ground. It's true, he thinks, that things have not been so good at home these days. That's for sure. But mostly that's been for all those other reasons, like Olga, who cries so much, her face just stays red and sweaty, and this even though Mami makes her special teas suggested by that curandera, the healer from across the line in Mexico. Mami even finally took Olga to a regular kind of doctor over here on the American side, who didn't know nearly as much as the curandera but charged a lot more, and he told Mami the baby had colic and that she'd better get used to the crying. Then Papi started staying out late again—not the whole night, like before when he had the girlfriend, but late enough so he didn't have to hear all that crying. Which, he said, he could not stand after he was working all day like a pinche burro, loading trucks for the Espinosa Brothers Shipping Company.

"Maybe it's because she's shy or something—that's why Tonantzin don't talk to you," Flaco says finally.

Riquis's eyes slowly slide back to him. "You saying I want that ugly thing to talk to me? That what you're saying?" His hands ball into fists as he talks.

"No, man, I know you don't like her." Flaco jumps back one step, never takes his eyes off Riquis, who is at least a head taller. He remembers what happened last week, after Riquis had been watching Tonantzin for more than two weeks: Riquis offered her a marshmallow cookie. Instead of looking at the cookie, she stared at Riquis's runny nose, so then he swiped at it with the back of his hand, which spread the snot across his face. This made her wrinkle up her own nose, like she smelled a fart, or maybe like she smelled Riquis, who most of the time pees the bed and kind of keeps that odor with him.

Then she shook her head and walked away, never even said a word. Just would not accept Riquis's stuff, like she was too good for his food, or something. Flaco has to admit to himself that this was pretty rude on her part, especially after making that face. Flaco nods as he thinks about it. "And why is she putting this curse on you?" he asks, wants to better understand.

Riquis shrugs and turns his eyes back to the cat. "Who knows why anything is? But think about it. Don't she always go into those hills?" He points his chin toward the deserted hills beyond Frontera Street. "There's nothing back there except lizards and snakes. And all normal girls are afraid of them, but this one, she goes back in there all alone, except for that cat. Think about it. Who likes cats? Uh-huh, witches."

"Sometimes we go back there."

"Not so far as her, stupid, and we go together for back-up. That one and her cat walk far into the hills, where no-body can see what they're doing. One time I saw she was carrying some kind of notebook and there was a pencil behind her ear. Probably for writing down the curses and things like that."

Flaco starts to say that maybe it's just homework. But Riquis's last sentence came out slow, each word measured, so he knows it's better to just shut up about the girl now. She should have accepted that cookie from Riquis, he thinks, and that's for sure.

Riquis loses interest in him now, bends his knees to a crouch, and rakes his hand across the dirt. His fingers curl around a rock as big as his fist and he brings his arm back in slow motion. The cat returns his stare. "You see," Riquis whispers, "that cat don't even blink, won't show me no respect." A second before Riquis throws the rock, it darts away.

Riquis stomps his feet and yells, "That's right, run, you coward. I'm the mero macho here." Then softer as he rubs the red chichón forming on his upper arm: "We'll meet up later, gato, now or in hell."

The next week, Flaco hangs upside down from the branch of a mesquite tree at the end of the street, just beyond the apartments. He's testing his ability to endure. As he does, his blood and thoughts pound inside his skull:

Better Riquis don't find out about this because his brother might think he's just doing it to challenge his position as the most macho of all boys in Mesquite Elementary School. He knows Riquis is not only the strongest—and Riquis will beat the shit out of anybody who says he isn't—but also he can eat the hottest peppers of anybody at the school. Hasn't he seen Riquis eat them little dried chile piquín like they was peanuts or something? And he knows that he, himself, is too skinny to beat the bigger boys in a fair fight, and there is no way he's going to pop them chiles. Once he tried and burned the skin right off his tongue. But he's sure that he can stay upside down longer than Riquis. There's no point telling him about it, though. Why get him all mad?

He is thinking that his eyeballs might pop out of his head from the pressure when he sees Tonantzin come out of her apartment, carrying that cat like it was a baby. From here he can't be certain, but it looks like it's got on a doll dress and a little hat like the pioneer girls wear in the cowboy movies.

He stretches his arms down until his fingers touch the ground, drops off the branch. He sways but stands still for a few minutes, until the dizziness goes away (probably set a record this time). Tonantzin faces the chain-link fence that cuts down the middle of Frontera Street.

A knot of people on the Mexican side push up against the fence, call out something to Tonantzin. He can't hear the words, but he doesn't have to. They're holding up jugs and buckets. They do this every year during the drought season when there's no more water left over there. He's not sure why they run out of water across the line when there's still some on this side, even if they do have to ration it; that's just the way it is every year. But nobody over here's allowed to give them water, because, like the radio disk jockey always says, "Hey, folks, our water level is low, too, so nobody can expect us to share with the Mexicans." Doesn't he have something there? Somebody's got to be left standing, Flaco figures, and it's better to be on the side of those who do have the water.

Tonantzin goes back inside her apartment now. When she comes out, she's pulling a long, black hose behind her instead of carrying the cat. Guess she doesn't know about the Border Patrol, he thinks, and starts scuffing down the dusty road, slow and casual, like he's not in a hurry to get down there where she is.

"Gracias, niña, gracias. May God bless you," the people say over and over again in Spanish. Tonantzin moves the hose from one container to another.

"You're going to get in trouble with the patrulla," he says. He stands back and to her side. Still casual-like, just passing by. "It's against the law, or something."

When Tonantzin shrugs her shoulders, pointy bones lift the material of her blouse. Skinny, that's what she is, he thinks, but now that he's looking up close (and he can pretty much stare because she's busy aiming that water and doesn't even look at him) he sees that her face isn't too bad, kind of pretty, even. She don't look even a little bit like a witch.

"Sometimes my mother and the other women give them water," he says, "but you got to wait until it's real dark. Even then, these days it's like the patrulla's got as many eyes as a centipede's got legs. I bet you they're going to be down here in that jeep in a few minutes. No joke. Next thing you know, they'll start saying you ain't got no papers to be here and drag you away and make all kinds of problems for everybody."

Tonantzin's cheeks glow red, but she just nudges the hose over to a gallon jug that a woman has in one hand while she holds a baby on her hip with the other hand. The baby stares at them with too-big eyes that move from Tonantzin to Flaco.

"You see," the woman says when she sees him looking at her baby. "Before when he cried, I would catch his tears with my finger and wet his little tongue with them, but now they're all dried up. We don't even have tears to drink."

He forces his eyes away from the baby, moves in closer now. What's wrong with this girl? Can't she hear so good? And why's she dancing from one foot to the other like she's got to pee or something?

He looks down: She's barefoot, and it's high noon. *Whew.* The ground's cooking right through the soles of his shoes, but there she is, enduring. She can take it like a man, that's for sure. It wouldn't surprise him if she pulled out a chile piquín right now and tossed it in her mouth; swallow a piece of hell just like it was nothing. Híjole.

For a second, he thinks of Riquis and what he would say, probably that it's just more proof that she's a witch. But witch or not, it takes huevos to walk on this earth with no shoes.

When he glances up, he sees she watches him and the corners of her lips twitch downward, but she stares him right in the eye, daring him to say something about her bare feet.

"You better stop," he says and makes a point of looking away from her feet. He figures she's probably saving her shoes for school, doesn't want them to wear out too fast, because El Kid Salazar isn't winning any fights and can't afford to buy her new ones. "I'm telling you, if the patrulla catches you doing this, it'll be the end of giving water."

The hose jerks, spills water onto the thirsty ground. Now she's listening.

"I can come around and get you tonight, if you want,"

he says. Funny how he never noticed that Tonantzin has this little birthmark—almost in the shape of a heart—under her right eye. "You know, in case you need some protection. But mostly to help with the hose and stuff."

It isn't easy to get the people at the fence to accept the plan. But he can see they understand they don't have any choice in the matter, so they keep their voices humble and say that they'll come back later. When he drags the hose back to Tonantzin's, he walks fast, without saying anything about it, so her feet don't get burned any more than they have to.

She stands blocking the door and he hands the rolled-up hose to her. "Your cat don't look too happy wearing them clothes," he says and laughs. The cat sits in the bedroom window, stares at them with its face in a frown.

"Her name is Estrellita," Tonantzin says and goes and gets the cat even though he's really not interested. "Pet her," she says when she comes back. "See how soft her fur is? And look," she says, points to its forehead, "you see, that's how she got her name, the little star, an estrellita."

She's also got a crossed eye, he thinks, but just nods and says, "Yeah, it's a good name for her." Then because he can't think of anything else to say, he turns away and waves to Tonantzin. "See you tonight," he says. He hesitates, starts to walk away, then turns to face her. "Better keep that cat inside."

When he turns the corner of the apartment building, Riquis, who is running out of their apartment, slams into him. "Got yourself a girlfriend, little brother? And don't lie, I seen you out the window, over there by the fence."

He grunts each time Riquis pounds him as they roll down the hill, legs wrapped around each other in the fashion of the hero wrestler, El Santo. His side scrapes, wedges against the side of a boulder. It happens so suddenly, he doesn't have time to take it like a man—instead, he screams in pain. Riquis quickly straddles his chest; his two legs squeeze both sides until Flaco gasps, breathes in the smell of dirty denim and pee.

Riquis grabs his wrists and pins his arms on the ground above his head. "Okay, give up, do you admit that I, El Gran Demonio, am greater than El Santo? Admit it or I'll crack your head open. Then I'll leave you here for the vultures to eat your brains. There they are, circling. Open your eyes and look at them; it's what's waiting for you. What, then, Mami's baby? You can't escape your fate. Go on, say the words: I accept my fate."

He releases one of Flaco's wrists to draw back his fist. Flaco flings his free arm across his face to wait for the blow. This time, he decides, he's determined to die before giving in. What was it their neighbor Joaquín was always talking about? Yeah, he remembers: It's better to die standing than to live kneeling. Wasn't that what Joaquín said somebody famous used to say? Well, he's ready. But Riquis better do it quick, get it over with before he changes his mind and starts begging like he usually does, because, what the hell, a dead man can't take his revenge.

He holds his breath, waits. Riquis's thighs relax; he slides off of him, moves to one side. Flaco peeks from beneath his arm and the afternoon sun almost blinds him. He opens his mouth, but Riquis clamps his hand over it, cuts his eyes to the top of the rock. Flaco rotates his shoulder from beneath the boulder, pushes himself to his knees, and looks.

A cat meows in the far distance. Riquis's head twists to the dirt road that comes up from Frontera Street and dead-ends into the sagebrush. "The witch," he whispers.

Below them, at the bottom of the hill, Tonantzin walks, now runs. "Estrellita," she calls. But the cat darts off through the sagebrush.

Tonantzin's brown hair waves down around her shoulders and glints red in the sunlight, little dots of fire dancing off her hair. She stands still now, her face lifted to the sun, her eyes closed. He glances at Riquis, who watches her with squinted eyes. All the while Riquis chews on his thumb, rips off the dirty nail with his teeth, spits it on the ground.

Tonantzin turns away, walks back toward the apartments. The cat suddenly reappears, prances out from behind a rock before it runs by Tonantzin's leg, brushes up against her as if it's teasing her, darts off, races her back to the apartments.

Riquis watches them until they disappear around the curve of the road.

Two days later, Riquis and Flaco lie flat, hug the swell of ground, peek over the rim from behind a cluster of maguey cactus, and watch Tonantzin. She cradles the bundle—a small object wrapped in a faded towel—in her arms and kneels before the grave that she dug earlier. There's a hole in the towel, and blood-matted gray fur pokes through. With her hand, she pushes her curtain of hair behind her ear.

He can see her face clearly, the eyes so puffy they're almost swollen shut, her nose red and runny. He remembers how the night before last, she'd looked different, smiled at him when they passed the water hose through the fence. He'd taken some of the marshmallow cookies for her to eat. That time she accepted them.

Now, both hands under the bundle, she lowers it into the ground. She makes the sign of the cross, then starts pushing the dirt into the hole. She's stopped crying now, but is still breathing through her mouth. He scoots down the slope, away from her, and rolls onto his back. Out of the side of his eye, he sees that Riquis watches him, but he doesn't return his gaze. Why doesn't she just leave now? What's she going to do, pray the whole rosary? He flops his arms over his eyes to protect them from the sun. A guy can go blind looking at such a bright light. He read that somewhere. He tries to think about the sun, the circle of light still burning on the inside of his lids; tries to concentrate on the hop-*whirring* of the grasshoppers in the dry weeds.

But it's no good. The memory of earlier today returns; he remembers it all: Papi didn't come home at all last night, so he and Riquis had run out right after their morning coffee and bread. They were in the back hill, not saying much, just looking down at their apartment door, each one alone with his own thoughts. The cat appeared, wore that doll's dress it had on the other time he'd seen it in the window. It spotted them and tried to run but got caught in the hem of the dress. It tripped, looked up, the small face turned a little to the side, that crossed eye staring right at him.

While it was tangled up in the material, Riquis drew back, rock in fist, and aimed. The cat yeowled. "Come on, pendejo," Riquis yelled at him, "get it while it's hurt." He just stood there and watched while Riquis ran at the cat, its blood a thin red line trailing in the dust behind it.

He turned away and ran home. Pues, what could he do? It was just a cat, after all. Fifteen minutes later, he sat on the rotten log in back of the apartments when Riquis returned, his chest bare, and held, with his two hands, a bloody mess balled up in his T-shirt.

"So, what do you think?" Riquis said, swinging it around, almost hit him in the face.

He turned his head away. So that's what death smelled like. He tightened his queasy stomach and said (watching Riquis's face now), "Know what I think? I think you're going to get it when Mami sees what you did to your shirt."

His words hit their target. Riquis put on his mean-guy face, but not before Flaco saw the fear go skimming across his eyes as fast as that cat used to run when it didn't have a dress on. For ruining his shirt, Riquis would get it with the leather belt hanging on a nail by the kitchen door. And for something as major as ruining clothes, Mami would soak the strap in water first.

Riquis shrugged, back to his former self now. "And what? She can't make me cry no more." His eyebrows pulled together like he was lost inside his head for a minute, then he said, "Anyway, it's worth it. The curse will lose its power now."

"Sure, sure."

Riquis kicks him in the side. "Toenail's gone," Riquis says. "Let's go dig it up." Flaco doesn't move.

"You turning chicken?" Riquis yanks Flaco's hair. "If you tell, you know what you're going to get."

"I don't snitch." He takes a deep breath, releases it, then pushes himself up from the ground. "I'm not digging it up," he says and keeps his eyes on the dusty tips of his shoes, toe to toe with Riquis's. He's surprised when the words don't come out as shaky as his knees. He takes another breath, holds it this time, tenses his muscles, and waits for the first punch. When nothing happens, he looks up.

Riquis watches him, studies his face. Finally Riquis shrugs, turns on his heel. "Well, I got a job to do," he says and starts toward the mound of dirt with the cross of sticks marking the head.

Flaco snatches up a sharp rock and jumps in front of Riquis. "Don't touch it, man, I ain't playing with you."

Riquis stops, stares him in the eye, but Flaco doesn't look away this time. Riquis stands so close he can feel his breath.

"Okay, okay," Riquis says, "don't act all crazy about it. I'm just saying we got to dig it up and burn it. That's what I should've done in the first place. That's why all the curse still isn't off."

"Man, you don't even know what you're talking about. Tonantzin ain't no witch, and that cat don't have nothing to do with no curse, neither."

"Then who's doing it, eh? Answer me that if you know so much."

Flaco shrugs. "Who knows why anything is?" he says. "It's all just shit, man."

Riquis narrows his eyes, and for a minute Flaco thinks he's had it. But then Riquis only kicks at the dirt. "Fuck you," Riquis says and turns, walks into the hills, away from the mound of dirt.

Flaco avoids looking at the grave, but that eye—the greenest he's ever seen—is right there inside his head, staring at him. He focuses on Riquis's back, still stiff from yesterday's whipping, and blood—little dots of red—seep through the faded blue of his T-shirt. Flaco walks behind him, but as he approaches Riquis, everything becomes slow motion: His brother floats inside a circle-haze of red that drifts slowly away, drifts away as slowly as a night without dreams.

The sun is playing tricks on him. He rubs his eyes, and when he opens them again, the haze lifts; there is only Riquis, walking faster now. Flaco runs to catch up, walk alongside his brother.

the girdle

EVEN THOUGH SHE STANDS ALONE, Amparo Sandoval, girdle clutched in hand, glances over her shoulder before she bends down in front of the kitchen sink. She lifts the curtain hanging from a straightened wire hanger, stuffs the time-stretched undergarment beneath a government-surplus cheese box in the garbage pail. When she straightens, she tilts her head to one side and strains to distinguish the sound that comes from the other side of the closed kitchen door.

No doubt Lázaro sits there: listening, spying. Now that he can no longer work and empty hours haunt him, she hoped he would go back to writing songs like those he used to sing to her. Then, the sweet-sad melody wrapped around her soul like a morning-glory vine, purple-blue spreading through her heart. Now she wants only for him to keep occupied, to stop following her every move, her every thought.

The rubber tires of Lázaro's wheelchair *squeak-squish* on the linoleum as it rolls away from the door. Amparo's hands close into damp fists. She swallows hard, turns the cold water spigot full force, soaks a rag, and holds it to her face.

Nine o'clock in the morning and already sweat trickles down her scalp. It's insane to wear a girdle during an

Arizona summer, she thinks, trying to form the explanation she will offer to Lázaro. Ever since their marriage, ten years ago, he has demanded that she wear a girdle the way any woman would when she no longer needs to lure a man. The first time he said this, she laughed, told him not wearing one had nothing to do with men. He slapped her face with the girdle, shouted that no one needed to tell him about the motives of women.

She knows now it is useless to explain. In truth, when her once-boy-slim body developed its feminine curves, she was proud and looked forward to the experience of life growing inside her. After the birth of her daughter, Teresita, her body grew fuller, softer, and the secret of creation filled her with a warm, white light that she couldn't quite explain. The glow of that light shone through her eyes, attracted others to her. Her spine seemed to extend, reach toward heaven like a supple, green stem. Men's eyes followed her, their challenged gazes like those in the pictures of the conquistadores who came to the Americas so long ago.

As she changed over the years, Lázaro's beatings became more severe and he insisted on increasingly stiffer girdles. Finally she told him that she had dreamed more than once that that piece of synthetic armor had stretched until it wasn't only her hips being bound, but her spirit; she wasn't able to breathe, to move—a live woman wrapped up like a mummy. Before she finished her sentence, he twisted her waist-length hair around his hand, slammed her forehead against the wall to remove her stupid thoughts.

Now she rubs the faint scar that ends above her right eyebrow and glances at the starburst clock on the wall. If she is to have time to see Manuel before going to work housecleaning for the Anglo couple, she must hurry. She eases open the door to the bedroom.

Lázaro sits in his chair in the center of the room, the once-feared hands now curved like broken talons in his lap. In October, it will be two years since the accident at the Espinosa Brothers Shipping Company that broke his back and stopped the beatings. He stares at her, dark eyes glittering, one side of his mouth twitching as if he knows something that he can't wait to spit out. He doesn't return her smile. For a second, fear sours her stomach, but she assures herself that it is only guilt making her silly. *It's only the girdle he's thinking about, he knows nothing about Manuel.*

She turns away, heads over to a chest of stacked wooden crates, but feels his eyes on her as she walks (muscles tense so her flesh won't move freely and enrage him). She painted the boxes black, as Lázaro insisted, rather than the pink their daughter had wanted. After picking up a hairbrush, she pauses, holds it in midair, before running it through her Yaqui-straight hair. Lázaro's breath rasps in his throat.

She steals a glance at his reflection in the scarred mirror above the chest. All the light has left his eyes, flat black disks following the movement of her arm. The blood drains from her heart even though she knows that familiar expression can no longer signal a pumalike lunge.

"Why did you take down the picture?" he says, finally.

"Picture?" she says, as if she doesn't understand, but her gaze slides to the crack in the wall the frame used to cover. On the advice of a curandera, she had, years ago, bought the special picture of the Virgin of Guadalupe. It was soon after she and Lázaro married, and he had already begun to accuse her of cheating even though she still adored him in those days. *The eyes of the Virgencita will follow him,* the curandera had said. *Lázaro will realize the purity of your devotion.* But in those days, Lázaro still walked tall, and the humble Virgin never lifted her eyes from the ground.

"Oh, that," Amparo says. "Hmm, I think maybe, yes, I remember, the nail came out last week. You know, it was loose, and I haven't had a chance to fix it."

"Don't give me none of your stories, puta. You don't want her eyes to follow you, verdad? Why is that, eh? What you got to hide? No, you don't want the Holy Mother looking at your shame, but you like to stare at yourself, don't you?" He is breathing through his mouth now. "Does he like to look at you, too?"

"Ay, Lázaro, why is God going to want to look at me?"

"Don't treat me like a pendejo." He's yelling now. "Not God. You know who I'm talking about, so don't give me that face of a saint. Look at me," he says and stares at his wasted lap. "Don't you think I got enough punishment, eh?"

"Don't start again. You don't know what you're saying." (But as she speaks, she thinks of Manuel crooning in her ear, "I want him to know you belong to me.")

Lázaro flops one hand at a time on the armrests of his chair, his eyes darting from one to the other as if the pain that darkens them could will strength into his arms and free him from his prison. The flaccid arms tremble, heave like a sigh, drop to his sides.

"Don't upset yourself," she whispers. "The doctor says it's not good for you."

"I'm a man. I'm . . ." As the words trail away, his body seems to collapse within itself: head sinks to chest, fingers curl back into palms.

She looks down, away, toward the stack of crates. From behind it, in its new position on the floor, between wall and box, one side of the framed picture sticks out. Amparo lifts her eyes, shifts her gaze, fixes her eyes on an alarm clock, its pulse regular and indifferent. For a moment she listens, almost hypnotized, then moves quickly toward Lázaro.

"Put your girdle on. I won't allow you to leave without it." His moist eyes meet hers for only a second before he lowers them. He reaches out and his fingertips flutter on her wrist, strong and brown beneath his pallor. "Don't go to work, forget the Anglo."

The nagging ache in her heart eases. "Mr. Ryan? I wish you could meet him, smell him, too, like cigars, really, it's true."

"Amparito, put it back on." His voice hasn't been so gentle since they first began dating when she was fifteen.

"Do you want the front window or the back today?" she says and moves behind his chair, grasps the handles. She looks down at the part in Lázaro's hair. Before, he smoothed it all back with brilliantine. But she combs it now, parted to the side and flattened with water—a hair-style for a serious man. Lázaro doesn't complain; he doesn't like to discuss the details of his appearance.

She glances at the clock. Manuel is waiting. Today she must give him an answer. "Like the song says," he told her last week, "it's now or never." He's leaving for Flagstaff in two weeks. Will she go with him? When he first asked her, she told him she needed time. But Manuel held on to her arm, his finger digging white spots into her flesh.

Now, when Lázaro doesn't answer, she rolls the chair into the kitchen, maneuvers it around the hole where the wooden floor has rotted. "There," she says and pulls back both panels of the plastic curtains before opening the window. "You can see the top of the hill, up there on Edwards Street, the pretty little houses."

She is the one who likes to gaze up at that neighborhood of individual houses with fenced yards, but it won't hurt him to look at her dream. Sometimes she tries to picture Manuel living in one of those houses, doing the wonderful family things that she imagines go on in middle-class families, like on the television programs Mrs. Ryan watches. For some reason, she can only picture Manuel in the bedroom—she and Manuel alone, arms and legs slippery-strong, intertwined in a passion that is better than tequila for blurring the day's reality.

Lázaro is looking out the window, his lips moving silently. He's praying, something he never did before. Sometimes, during the night, he screams out for God to stop the pain.

Amparo moves to the side and sees that Lázaro is staring straight ahead. She squints her eyes against the sun's light and looks out at the desert-brown hill—a steep climb, but not too difficult for a strong person—that leads up to Edwards Street. The air is still, and the dry brush and scrubby mesquite trees don't sway. Teresita sits at the bottom of the hill, playing with her dolls, wraps them tightly in rebozos. As she pretends to drink coffee from little cups, her child-large eyes glance behind, over her shoulder: Lázaro always warns her to be careful on that hill. It only looks calm, he says; tarantulas and scorpions wait below in dark places.

A slight breeze that seems to come from nowhere touches the mesquite branches. The hot, dry air carries the odor of dog, so that Amparo smells the animal before she sees it. It edges around the corner of the building, large head hanging low. It walks slowly—protruding bones that seem to move in some ancient harmony—toward a cardboard box of trash to Teresita's right.

"No," Lázaro calls out. The dog stops, turns its yellow eyes toward him. With each pant, its thirst-swollen tongue lolls farther out the side of its mouth. "Do you hear, woman?" Lázaro whispers. "It calls my name. Listen. Lázaro, it says. Lázaro." He tries to laugh but manages only a dry rattle low in his throat. He presses back into his chair.

Amparo runs to the kitchen door, shouts at Teresita to move, then picks up a rock and throws it. The dog flinches. With age-yellowed teeth, it pulls the newspaper-wrapped bundle from the box before running up the hill. Midway it pauses and shakes the bundle until the paper falls away. It grasps the inner contents and runs. A ribbon of gauze unfurls behind it. It is the bandage that had wrapped Lázaro's bedsores, memories he brought when they sent him home from St. Jude's charity ward. *Nothing more we can do for you,* the blunt Mother Superior had told them. *No point in wasting the money of others. Go home, pray. Endure your wait like a man. It won't be long.*

Now the dog lies at the top of the hill and chews on one end of the bandage. A long finger caked with the blood and pus of Lázaro's life, it trails down the hill, points toward the apartments. The dog works its jaws and stares at them. Teresita returns to her dolls and empty cups.

When Amparo returns to Lázaro's side, he mutters, "Did you hear it? Did you hear it call my name?"

"Don't talk crazy," she says, even though she, too, heard something. She straightens Lázaro's collar, tells him their neighbor Joaquín will come over later to look in on him. "If I don't go now, I will lose my job." She turns, walks back into the bedroom for her purse, continues on through the front, living room during the day, Teresita's bedroom at night. After she unlatches the hook on the screen door, she pushes it open and steps outside. The blast of oven-hot air scorches the sweet odor of sickness and decay from her nostrils.

"Why does a woman stop wearing a girdle, eh, Amparo?" Lázaro yells at her back. "That's what I want to know."

Without turning around, she stops: Maybe the girdle isn't so important, after all. If it will make him feel better . . . well. Should she dig it out of the trash?

The door thumps softly as it closes behind her. She shakes her head no.

Once she is out of sight, her stride lengthens and grows increasingly surer as she walks up the dirt road that leads away from Frontera Street to downtown Mesquite. Lázaro has always forbidden her to return to school, but last week she stopped by the Santa Cruz Business College and picked up brochures and an application. Once she becomes a secretary, she'll move from the apartments on Frontera Street, rent a stucco bungalow, maybe even on Edwards Street. She and her daughter will celebrate birthdays with pink-frosted cakes, and on Christmas they'll string tiny bulbs around the windows and doorways. Light and laughter will bounce through the house like a child's rubber ball. She'll buy new furniture—not really new, of course, but Soto's Used Furniture sometimes has some nice items in their display window. And there will be no one to gamble the furniture away in a poker game.

It occurs to her that she doesn't know how much poker Manuel plays. There are many things she doesn't know about him.

By the time Manuel's taxi on Main Street comes into her sight, her cotton blouse, the material thin from many scrubbings, clings to her. She digs out a wad of bathroom tissue from her purse and dabs at the perspiration on her neck and between her breasts. Tiny pearls of paper stick to her damp skin.

Manuel slouches behind the steering wheel of his poppy red Chevy, parked in the shade of a mesquite tree. His head lifts and turns slightly to the right as he looks in the rearview mirror and spots her. After easing the car out of its space, he slowly drives past the Mesquite Bus Depot and into the alley off Main where she is to meet him.

As she watches him, she thinks about the emotions that always engulf her when he kisses her. His need, so intense it never ceases to startle her, makes her dizzy with the realization that her nearness could stir up so much desire. But her feelings of power last only seconds. As his kiss deepens and his hands move more urgently, the world around her becomes less real, an emotional whirlpool carrying her down and away from herself.

A drop of sweat plops onto her eyelashes. She blinks it away and stares at the dark entrance to the alley. She can almost breathe in, taste the Sen-Sen and cigarette tobacco on Manuel's breath; feel the oddly smooth, honey gold skin beyond the weathered *V* on his chest. She tries to take a deep breath, but she cannot. It is as though she were wearing her girdle, wrapping tighter, tighter.

She closes her eyes and tries to picture Manuel in a house of cotton-candy pink. She cannot. She glances at the sun, its ascent steady and sure in the cloudless sky. It's now or never, she thinks.

Later that day, Amparo sits at her kitchen table, relaxing now that the dinner dishes have been put away and Teresita has been bathed and tucked in at one end of the worn sofa. She listens to romantic songs on the radio while one finger traces a faded vine in the oilcloth. Her other hand, still burning from Mrs. Ryan's cleaning chemicals, wraps around a soda bottle. The coolness eases the ache in her palm, and when she drinks the dark, sweet liquid, her thirst is lessened for a moment.

Lázaro moans from the bedroom, calls out, "Can't you have a little respect? How's a man supposed to sleep with that noise?"

She knows it is not the radio keeping him awake—he cannot tolerate silence since he returned from St. Jude's. They both understand.

"The Virgencita is back in her place," he says. "I asked Joaquín to do it. You didn't notice."

Amparo gets up, walks to the doorway between the rooms, looks in on Lázaro. "I noticed," she says, her voice lowered to a whisper that will not awaken Teresita. She had felt the presence of the returned image as soon as she walked into her apartment earlier. Though, in truth, the long-suffering eyes had never left her. Amparo glances back at the curtained kitchen sink, the small gray heap the girdle makes on the floor where it has been pulled out of the garbage. "You have been busy today," she says.

They both are silent for long moments, then in a voice distant and singsong, Lázaro begins to reminisce about their life before the accident and how things hadn't been that bad, had they?

The drone of his litany hypnotizes Amparo, and her thoughts drift back to earlier in the day and Manuel. When she reached the alley opening, she had paused for only a second. Even though she sensed Manuel watching her, she began to cross to the other side, stumbled on a broken bottle, stopped only long enough to kick the jagged shards out of her way. On the sidewalk once more, she walked faster, faster, broke into a run. Away from Manuel. Her heart felt as if it were being squeezed by a giant fist, but she was afraid that if she stopped she might turn back.

"Remember when I took you flowers and serenaded?" Lázaro says. "I wrote songs for you; many times you helped me find the words. And you always had a nice voice. You don't sing no more, Amparito."

"And you don't write songs no more. Those things happened a long time ago, Lázaro."

"Does that mean they didn't never happen?" he says.

Amparo turns back to the kitchen, gazes at the starburst clock. "It's late. I'm going to take out the garbage now."

"And your girdle?" Lázaro's voice is soft, resigned.

"Ya sabes, you already know," Amparo says as she walks away. She drops the girdle back into the small pail beneath the sink. Outside, she empties the trash into a large aluminum can she bought at the hardware store today. At least it will allow Lázaro to pretend the dog can be kept away—perhaps then he will not fight sleep. What can this small illusion hurt? she thinks. It will be for such a short time. She can wait.

Memories in White

DON ALFONSO HEARS HIS DAUGHTER, Irene, call him, just as she did in his dream last night, but he does not answer. He can't find his gold pocket watch in the dresser drawer, and he's not leaving without it. A gift to himself, years ago, after his company's first successful season, the watch loses time now. But when he slips it into the vest pocket of his white linen suit, he can almost believe that he is once again El Palomo Blanco, the White Dove.

"Papi," Irene repeats, voice *nick-nicking* at the other side of the adjacent wall. "We don't want to be late, I made reservations. And your friend can't stay too long, remember?"

"Yes, yes," he says, drums his fingertips on the dresser, *1–2–3–4.* This luncheon was her idea. She told him about it almost the moment he stepped off the plane three days ago, said they'd go out, just the two of them, after her children returned to university. *Time for us to talk,* she said. About what? he wondered silently, and suggested he would like some of his business associates from the old days to join them. She said nothing at first, but finally agreed to invite his friends. After making calls, she told him that of all the group, only Eusebio Ruiz was still living. If there could be only one, he was thankful it was Ruiz. So much like him, brothers of the soul.

In the old days, the muchachos—Ruiz in particular, if he remembers correctly—always admired his watch. Don Alfonso presses his palms onto the dresser top, covers the space within his hand's span, touch-searches. What's this? A rectangular cardboard box, and still packed inside, the vanity set Irene gave him when he first arrived at her home in Mesquite. *After Jorge operates on your cataracts,* she had said, *you'll regain your vision. Then when you return to México, every time you see yourself in this mirror, you'll remember us.*

Irene, Don Alfonso thinks, is as sentimental as her mother was during the early years of their marriage. Why would a man of his age want to accumulate more things? Why would he want to be confronted by the reflection of a face lost to time? And anyway, he did not tell Irene that he would definitely allow her husband, Dr. Lapuente, to operate. He only said *maybe.* In truth, he has no interest in removing the Vaseline-like haze from his eyes, prefers to remember the world as it was, not as it has become.

What's this next to the box? A bottle, small and ornate. He brings the flask to his nose. Even without lifting the stopper, the cloying sweetness of flowers, decay, death invades his nostrils. He draws back his head sharply, returns the perfume to its place.

He sighs and thinks of how Irene doesn't have her mother's gift for organization. Beatrice. His wife of how long? Forty years? Forty-five? A perfect companion once she learned to understand his needs—so efficient she made it seem as though things ran effortlessly, so loyal and unobtrusive that, until she died, he could almost forget she existed. He shakes his head gently, dry leaves of memory skitter-scattering through his mind.

"Are you okay in there?" Irene calls, follows her voice into his room.

"Ready to leave," he says and means it because his

groping hands have found his pocket watch hanging from the edge of the dresser mirror. (Now he remembers how he left it there to keep the chain from tangling.) He fumbles as he attaches the chain to his vest.

"Here, permit me," Irene says.

"This, at least, I can still do for myself. Or are you like your brother that you think I am old and useless?" he says, tightens his grip on the watch.

"I only want to help."

"According to Samuel, I'm no longer capable of managing my own company," he says. "I, the man who started it, built it up."

She doesn't answer, just as he thought she wouldn't. His children treat him as if his mind were as decrepit as his body has become. They expect him to believe that he is being forced into retirement so he can enjoy life. As if life without work ever meant anything.

Irene's hands tremble, hesitate, before she lifts them from his, slide up to straighten his tie. "How handsome you look in your new suit, Papito," she says. "The years can't touch you, always so dignified, formal. Everyone is still captivated by your Old World charm." She pats her hand lightly over his heart, *rap-rap, rap-rap*. "Always the same," she says. "You never change."

"Hmmph," he grunts, but is pleased with her words in spite of the hint of long suffering that curdles the edges and must be ignored. Before he left Guadalajara, he had insisted that his son, Samuel, take him to the tailor's, have them make this suit to his exact specifications. During his younger days, as a successful businessman, he wore white linen while in the hotter regions: Sinaloa, Sonora, Arizona. The women always complimented him on his looks, and now Irene's flattery allows him to feel like himself again and his stomach relaxes.

"They used to call me El Palomo Blanco, remember?" he says.

Irene drops her hand and steps back away from him. She hesitates then, her tone more serious than he expected, says, "How could I forget? That was when you still had the regional office just across the border. You let us come and stay with you for a while." Another pause. "I've been thinking about those days myself. It's one of those things we need to talk about."

What does she mean, *need* to? Such an aggressive woman, he thinks, and silently blames her behavior on years of living in the United States, of adopting the demanding ways of the gringas. But no, now that the novelty of seeing Irene again after six years has worn thin, he's beginning to remember that those tendencies always existed in her, and how he was relieved when her visits to his home in Guadalajara dwindled to nothing. She only recently resumed the once-weekly phone calls—consisting of more pauses than words—finally inviting him here so her husband, the ophthalmologist, could operate on his eyes.

Even as a little girl she was pesky, a tune that sticks in the mind, interrupts logic. In those times, when she disturbed his peace, Beatrice would lead her away—a whining, pouting child, eyes accusing him. Of what? What did she want from him? He had his work to think of, after all. And, too, how much could he say to a girl? He expected her only to be pretty, clever, but in a feminine way. Her brother was the one he had to prepare for taking over the family business, although he did not expect this to be during his own lifetime. Samuel was the older child and the only male. Well, no, he corrects himself, there was the other one, but there's no point in thinking about that. He rotates fingertips to temples.

"Are you all right?" Irene says.

He nods, mumbles it's only a slight headache, but apparently she thinks she knows better. "You look so tired," she says. "Jorge and I heard you last night—you were having a bad dream, a nightmare, I think. I opened your door and watched you, but you settled down." When he doesn't respond, she adds, "What was it about?"

"It's nothing," he says, irritated that not only has she invaded the privacy of his bedroom while he was sleeping, but now she wants to poke around in his mind. "Dreams have no significance," he says. "I give them no importance."

He doesn't tell her that the nightmares come regularly now and always the same: visions of churches, shadows he can't make out, wisps of incense smoke drifting up to be lost in the darkness of high ceilings. Distant voices calling, hissing his name, yanking him from his sleep. When he thought he would die from lack of rest, he had his doctor prescribe pills. They do render him unconscious, but it seems to him that it becomes increasingly difficult to wake up, escape the dreams. Everyone told him he needed a vacation, a change of scenery. And so he accepted Irene's invitation, had finally become excited about the prospect of returning to his past, a time that seems less and less real to him.

Now he's beginning to understand that coming here has been a bad idea. It's true that he spent his best days in this region; his negotiating skills in business were well known. But if he thought he would be able to recall the man he was then, well, so far those memories remain as illusive as time itself. It seems to him that Ruiz is the key. If their memories meet, blend, then maybe he can convince himself that the man he thought he was did exist.

"I'm late," he says. "Ruiz is waiting."

Irene presses his walking cane into his right hand, pushes her palm into the small of his back, and guides him to her Cadillac outside. Don Alfonso listens for Irene to turn the ignition, for the subsequent silence that finally overcomes her while she is driving. She has not lost her mistrust of machines, and he knows she will give the automobile her full concentration.

When he was younger, he liked all things mechanical, though lately he has lost interest in keeping up with the newer inventions. One knows where one stands with machines, he thinks. Hadn't he learned the dangers of emotions, of what can happen to a heart that loves too much? He had adored his father, yet all his feeling couldn't prevent his parents from being killed in a robbery, nor had love served as good training for the life that awaited him at the St. Joseph orphanage. But he'd learned to make his way alone. At least he made certain his children had everything: a successful father, a dutiful mother, a house so full of art objects, visitors said it resembled a museum. He has provided for his family. This no one can deny.

Pulling a handkerchief from his pocket, he dabs at his mouth, at the moisture beading beneath the carefully waxed mustache, and tells himself it is too much free time that fills his head with pointless reminiscences. If he doesn't watch out, he'll soon be playing Beatrice's favorite role as martyr. Don Alfonso leans back against the seat, closes his eyes, turns his face into the stream of air-conditioning that keeps at bay the blazing desert heat. He'd forgotten how merciless the desert sun could be.

Don Alfonso takes off his Panama hat when he steps into the restaurant, smooths back his still-plentiful hair. He brings up the back of his hand to his nose, presses as if to keep out the air. "It smells like a funeral parlor in here," he says.

"Ay, Papi, this is my favorite restaurant. It's lovely, I

thought you'd like it. You should see, vases of lilies, gladiolus, carnations everywhere."

He recalls the Montezuma Lounge he and the muchachos used to frequent: There, a haze of cigar smoke drifted through almost tangible odors of beer, whiskey, leather upholstery, all wrapping around him like a father's embrace in the cave-dark room. "Too much light," he says.

Irene asks if he would like her to have some blinds closed. He waves his hand. "Yes, yes," he says and can't help once again comparing Irene to her mother. Beatrice would have noticed the light and taken care of it without burdening him with details.

Irene leads him to the table. Round and draped with a moon-white cloth, it seems to glow, stare at him, an eye, large, unblinking. He can make out no human forms waiting. Irene pats his hand as though he were a child, tells him she'll call Ruiz if he doesn't arrive shortly, but meanwhile, don't they have a wonderful opportunity for a private conversation? She orders wine for herself, milk for his stomach. Once it arrives, she clears her throat, says, "Well, here we are, father and daughter."

Don Alfonso understands Irene's invitation has been about more than cataracts, but he says nothing as she gulps her wine. He waits, drums on the tabletop, *1–2–3–4, 1–2–3–4,* imagines her sitting across from him, watching him, her bottom lip stuck out in that ridiculous little-girl pout. Who could have patience with such silliness?

"I've been thinking about when we were all together as a family," she says finally. "You, Mamá, me, Samuel, and poor little Gabrielito," she says. "When you had the office in Sonora. He was born right across the border, buried there, remember?" Her words grow soggy, sentimental with the wine.

"Of course," he says. "I'm not an imbecile." A slight flutter in his chest, far away. He takes a deep breath, the way his doctor instructed him to do, thinks of something pleasant. "It was then they gave me my nickname."

"Yes," Irene says, pauses to pour herself more wine.

When she begins to speak again, he interrupts, senses something in the tone of her voice, some hint that she plans to distort the memory. That, he will not allow. After all, it happened to him, not her. "I remember the day distinctly," he says and begins to tell the story.

So long ago, in Sonora. He had just closed a deal with Santiago Fine Furniture, unloaded all those expensive French bedroom suites from his inventory for a hefty profit. Afterward he met with the manager of some large hotel about an Italian chandelier he had in stock, perfect for the lobby. He knew Beatrice would already be waiting in the car for him, as planned, at the foot of the Church of the Sacred Heart. He was late, but she would understand. She always did.

Irene and Samuel were with her; perhaps he'd promised to take them to dinner or something. The sun—a bone-bleaching white that day, as white as the suit he wore—beat down at his back as he crested the hill on which the small church sat. As he started down the wide steps, he looked into the eyes of a flower vendor at the end of the path. Her dark eyes watched him from beneath the shade of her hand. "Look, look," she called, perhaps to the other vendors or to no one in particular. "A palomo blanco, a white dove. He's flying out of the sun."

He was accustomed to admiring looks and words. But he remembers how the image the vendor's words created stopped him for a second. Now he says nothing to Irene about the thought, that day, that swept down as silent as a moth's wings, tried to slip in the back door of his mind. But it didn't quite get through, just as it won't today. If someone had asked him to explain his reaction to her words, he couldn't have; he only knew that his eyes burned as if a tear wanted to form, and for a moment he couldn't see where he was going. He blinked and his vision returned to normal. He spotted the car below and hurried his step.

As he approached the vendor, she tossed flowers in his path and called out, "Flowers for the Palomo Blanco." She giggled and he smiled at her attentions, but the moment's importance had passed for him; his mind had gone on to organize topics to be covered during the conference he had the next day.

"White carnations," Irene says now.

"How's that?"

"White carnations," she repeats. "That's what kind of flowers they were." Alcohol has softened Irene's words, and they slide out smooth, soft, riding on a scarf of silk.

He imagines a bolt of scarlet cloth unwinding, wrapping around his head, his face, and is suddenly reminded of some long-dead American dancer. What was her name? The crazy one who Beatrice admired so much, Duggan, Duncan, something like that. Wasn't the woman killed in her car when she became entangled, blinded by scarves?

"How beautiful you were that day in your white suit and the sun at your back," Irene says. "It caught the gold in your hair, a halo of sunshine around your head."

Don Alfonso closes his eyes, nods.

"Alone, as usual," she continues, "shining in your own light. The vendor threw flowers. Everyone loved you then. When you got in the car, the scent of carnations clung to the soles of your shoes."

He breathes in deeply and smells the sweet-spice scent of the memory.

How strange that he should forget such a detail when now it seems so vivid, so overpowering, suffocating. He has breathed in something else along with the scent of flowers. Hate?

His lungs ache. "I am very tired," he says. "Better call Ruiz. If he's not coming, why stay?"

"Forget Mr. Ruiz," Irene says, her voice full of forced cheer. "We'll order lunch, all your favorites. Just listen how we're finally talking to each other."

"Forget? Is he coming, yes or no?"

She pauses, says, "His granddaughter called this morning. He's too sick—"

"Why didn't you say so?" he says, interrupting. "We could have gone to him."

Irene sighs. "Papi, to be honest, when I called, his granddaughter gave him your name and he couldn't remember you. Mr. Ruiz, well, his mind is all mixed up, doesn't know what's real anymore. Just imagine, he thinks his granddaughter is his sister, argues with her about some childhood rivalry. They say he always confuses the dead with the living, as if ghosts from the past were the only true reality. I just didn't have the heart to tell you."

Don Alfonso presses the tips of his fingers together, a steeple, one hand against the other. "I am ready to leave," he says and stands.

At Irene's house he takes off his jacket, insists on lying down. "Just a headache," he says and pushes Irene's hands away when she tries to tuck a comforter around him. She leaves, returns with a glass of water that he has requested for his sleeping pill, and more wine for herself.

"I'm surprised you remembered the name of the church, you know, where the flower woman gave you your nickname." She sips. "Do you remember it's where Gabrielito was baptized? The funeral Mass was there, too. His tiny casket beneath a blanket of white carnations, the scent never leaves me. You weren't able to make it for that, of course."

He had forgotten it was the same church, but, yes,

she's correct. Beatrice became obsessive about that place, attending Mass there every day, not wanting to leave, until the doctors feared for her sanity. So for her sake, he gave up a lucrative office, returned them all to Guadalajara. Didn't he do his best? Why does Irene insist on staining his memories with her faraway sorrows?

"You didn't remember," she says.

"*Remember, remember,*" he repeats. "Is that the only word you know? Of course I do. But what is the point of going on and on about the dead? Is this why you invited me here? To bring up your past?"

"Ay, Papi, I only want to talk about him. So beautiful he was, like a little doll. Mamá never recovered from his death."

Don Alfonso rubs his forehead. "Life is for the living."

Irene laughs, forced, high-pitched, and Don Alfonso thinks of how there is nothing more unattractive than a drunk woman. "Life is for the living," Irene repeats. "That's what you told Mamá when you didn't make it for the funeral."

"I tried to make it back," he says. "Is it my fault the plane was delayed?"

"But you could have come sooner, when she first called, told you Gabriel was sick and she feared he was dying."

"In those days your mother was prone to hysterics. How was I to know the child was truly ill? I'm not a doctor. I was in the middle of an important business meeting when she called." He slips his watch from his pocket as he talks, rubs his thumb over the time-etched surface, realizes the ticking has stopped. In all this excess emotion, he has, for the first time, forgotten to rewind.

"Didn't you ever love anybody, Papi?" She's crying now, words sloshing in tears and wine, and Don Alfonso sees that she is more like her mother than he had realized.

Although Beatrice, at least, kept her thoughts to herself and her bottle of brandy.

"Oh, I see," he says. "You brought me here to make accusations. Well, you have made them. Now I must rest." He wants to end it there, to brush her aside, but somehow feels he must make his side more clear. "I had others depending on me, you know—a wife, Samuel, you." He ticks them off on his fingers, *1–2–3*.

He turns his head to the wall, crosses his arms across his chest. He has nothing more to say. She sits on the bed a few minutes longer, finally pushes up with a sigh. But as she walks away, she says, "But don't you ever even think of him?"

"Where's the logic?" he says and closes his eyes. "Regrets change nothing, better to push those things from your mind. It's a lesson I learned long ago." He waits to hear the door close behind her, waits for the pill to take effect.

Finally, darkness envelops him and he is thankful. But the blankness is not complete; a pinpoint of light in the distance. It whispers his name, echoes down to him on a weak beam that grows, expands until light wraps around him, binds him in a cocoon of white. A sudden wind howls behind him, catches him, whirls him through a tunnel stretching out as long as time. He stirs, groans, wills himself to awaken, but he cannot.

The light becomes brighter still, blinds him, and he senses a presence. He shades his eyes, squints at the looming shadow: a church, its door a heart, red, throbbing blood onto the pavement, ribboning down the steps to where he stands. *Drip-drip, drip-drip*. The sun, white-hot, is melting him, and he knows he must get into the cooling darkness. He presses his face against stained-glass windows, images of Madonna and child.

"Wake up, wake up," Don Alfonso croaks into the emptiness of his room, but the dream holds tight.

From the interior of the church, a voice, a whisper. He strains to hear, yearns for the comfort of his mother's voice in lullaby. *Alone,* it says, *alone in your own light.* The words pull him inside against his will, and shafts of barb-tipped darkness wheeze, whistle by, then return to wrap around him.

He presses his hands over his ears, squeezes his eyes shut. "Let me out, out," he says, words forced between fitful moans. And once again he is outside the stone walls. A rebozo-wrapped crone creeps out of the church shadow and into his light, clutches at him.

Alms, alms for the poor, she says.

Let me go, he says, but she clasps tighter still.

We love you, she says, holds on with both hands, tries to pull him to her. *Love you,* she repeats. A refrain, *tick-tock, tick-tock.* She lifts her head, dark eyes directed up at him, wells of blackness swallowing light. The rebozo drops away. Face contorting, transforming: Beatrice, Samuel, Irene, everyone he ever knew. Gabriel smiling, lips pulling back, tighter, rotting, flesh falling away, only a black hole remains.

Movement deep inside the void. A flutter; legs, spindle-thin, reaching up, clutching at the edge, climbing out. The moth emerges, hesitates for only a second before it escapes, flies away toward the light.

Always in your own light, a voice calls after the moth. Don Alfonso's heart beats faster, faster against the bars of his rib cage, and he almost awakens. Not yet, he thinks. Keep the dream a while longer. It's almost finished. Gossamer wings flap, scatter time. The moth disappears into the light, gives itself up to its destiny. *Love you, love you,* words strewn like ashes in the wind.

Don Alfonso's breath comes easier now, his eyelids lift. Irene's shadow covers him. She clinches his shirt in her hands. "Wake up, Papi," she says.

He is grateful when she doesn't cry saying good-by at the airport, only embraces him. She doesn't release him immediately, holds on, presses her cheek against his chest, whispers to his heart, "I love you."

"Yes, yes," he says finally, "me too. But now I must hurry."

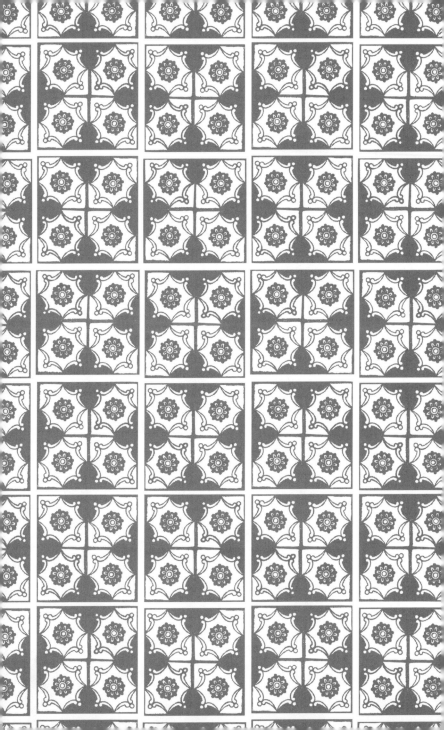

blanca rosa

Cisco López leans against the outside wall of the Mesquite Bus Depot and, through half-closed eyes, watches the Greyhound bus pull to the curb. He yawns, vaguely wonders how many passengers will get off here in Arizona and how many will continue on across the border into Mexico. Suddenly he straightens. The Lucky Strike drops from his stained fingers.

"Hey, vato, qué pasa?" Paquito Murphy says. "You look like you seen a ghost."

Cisco doesn't answer. He looks beyond the others leaving the bus to where she stands at the top of the steps. The path finally clears, and as she descends, a dying ray of afternoon light reveals a complexion as smooth as a river-worn stone. She is young, maybe sixteen.

When she steps onto the sidewalk, something sparkles—a circlet of rhinestones glitters around her ankle. The row of tiny glass cubes winks at him, almost hypnotizes him as she walks to the side of the bus and waits for the attendant to unload her luggage. When, out of the corner of his eye, Cisco catches the movement of a man to his side, he quickly steps forward. He moves toward her, his pace not so fast that other men hanging around the bus station on nothing-to-do Sundays will laugh, but not so slow that it

73

would allow one of them to get to her first. "Señorita," he says and bows slightly at the waist to demonstrate his honorable intentions. "Please permit me to help you."

When the stranger turns, their eyes are level. He blinks. Ojos moros, Moorish eyes, but something wrong: It is the color, so dark that for a moment the irises seem to be without pupils, like there's no way to get in, everything locked inside. And in spite of the dry heat of the Sonoran desert, a slow chill, like a distant memory, prickles his mind. She lowers her gaze and smiles and he loses his thought in the deep dimple that forms in her cheek.

Suitcase in hand, he walks her to the depot entrance and holds the glass door open with his free hand. He refuses to acknowledge Paquito, who watches with his cow eyes and brushes against Cisco's arm as he slides through the door before the woman. He breathes in her scent: floral soap with just a trace of sweat.

Inside, strains of Javier Solis's "Gema" crackle from the plastic radio on top of the row of metal lockers. "Beautiful song, no?" he says and hopes she will look up and read in his expression that he dedicates this song to her, his newfound precious gem. But her eyes focus on something far away.

He sets down the suitcase and wipes his sweaty palms on his jeans before extending his hand. "Forgive my lack of manners. I'm Francisco López, your servant." He introduces himself in Spanish, the language he spoke with his mother.

She lifts her eyes briefly before looking to the side. "Blanca Rosa del Río."

"Blanca Rosa," he repeats and thinks how well the name, White Rose, suits her. "Roses, they were my mother's favorite. You see?" He points to the tattoo on his bicep. A full-petaled rose begins at the top of his arm, and on the lip of one petal the word *Madre* is written in script. The triangular head of a snake rests to the side of the bloom, while the serpent's body coils around the length of the long stem; thorns prick at its flesh, leaving a trail of ink-blue droplets of blood.

"And you like snakes also?" Blanca Rosa asks with a small smile.

He shrugs and glances toward the soda fountain. He planned on offering her a Coke, but he sees Paquito already there, watching, straddling the stool, back against the counter, thumbs hooked in pants pockets. "I'll be back," Cisco says to Blanca Rosa before walking toward Paquito. Cisco balances on the edge of the stool next to Paquito, faces the opposite direction, says in a low voice, "What're you looking, eh, cabrón?"

"I'm only waiting to see if you want to forget about that job de pendejo you have and make some real money this weekend. Pues, we was talking about that earlier."

"Yeah, and what did I told you?" Cisco stands up. "When I left L.A. I told you now I'm coming home, la vida loca is finished for me."

"Ay, hombre, you came back because your mother died—and I understand that—like a saint, your mother." Paquito holds up his hands, palms outward. "But me and you, we ain't never gonna be players. Gotta face up, mi carnal—we was born to ride the wind like them tumbleweeds." He indicates the outside with his chin.

"You don't know nothing." When he steps closer to Paquito, Josie the waitress walks over to the counter, cuts her "I been working two shifts, so don't give no problems" eyes at them, and Cisco turns away.

Back at Blanca Rosa's side, he says, "Do you have the time to take a little walk?" So that she won't be afraid, he pulls out his driver's license, shows he has not lied about his identity, and promises her that they will stay outside where others can see them. He makes a walking motion with two fingers, says, "We can go to the plazita."

With her eyebrows knitted, she squints at the plate-glass window where the words, seen backward from the inside, read, Welcome to Mesquite. "Yes, why not? I plan to stop in Mesquite."

They stroll into the oncoming twilight toward the plaza; he walks on the outside, hand cupping her elbow when they cross the street. Her arm is tense and her eyes are now less far away, more alert, watching. Is she afraid of him and the strange surroundings? "You're more delicate than your name," he says gently, hopes to assure her she is safe. He wants to add that she is his dream realized, but decides to hold that for later.

Suddenly she throws her head back and laughs, a short, barklike sound. "Tell me," she says, "do you think that flowers should be left to live in the outdoors?" She makes an expansive gesture with her arms. "Or should they be picked and kept indoors so only some can appreciate them—even if it means the flower will wilt and die much sooner?"

He is fascinated with her doll-like face and something more he can't define, so he gives her the answer he thinks will please her. "Let them grow free like God meant. That way, all the world can enjoy their grace." When she slips back into silence, he clears his throat, says, "Many people come to Mesquite for the good weather—or to cross the border into México." He hopes she will say what has brought her.

"Why is the snake choking the flower?" She touches the rolled-up sleeve of his T-shirt.

"Choking? It's only a tattoo, it means nothing."

"Now you're angry with me." She pouts like a little girl and they both laugh.

In the plazita, he watches her as she leans forward on the edge of a park bench, head tilted, as if listening to the coos of the mourning doves. He wants to continue that way: Blanca Rosa as serene as a porcelain figurine, he by her side. Although he doesn't like that her odor of sweat has become stronger—almost offensive—after their walk. Blanca Rosa swings her leg out, interrupts the tranquillity, rhinestones glimmering in the growing shadows.

"Where did you get that?" he says and indicates the anklet with a jerk of his head.

"It's nothing, a gift. You don't like it?" She stretches out her leg. "I always have problems with the catch."

He kneels in front of her, bends over in order to see. The warm, earthy scent of woman meets him. Maybe this girl isn't so pure after all, he thinks, and his eyes avoid the darkness between her opened legs. But when he glances up at her, her large eyes are unfocused, seeing something that is only within her scope of vision. She isn't trying to seduce him, he decides, doesn't even seem aware of him. His hands shake and he thinks he will have to break the chain, but finally it loosens and falls off into his palm. He rubs the faint impression it has left on her skin.

He stands up and drops the anklet into his jeans pocket. "You need to rest, Blanquita," he says. "My pickup is on the next block. We can go back to the depot and get your bag, and then, with your permission, I'll take you to your family."

"I have no one," she says.

"No one? You mean in Mesquite?"

"I'm alone in Mesquite, alone everywhere," she whispers, her voice drifting up like fog. With a slow waving motion of her hand she says, "Like a river, flowing, flowing away." He smiles: It is like a scene from a melodramatic Mexican movie.

"Does your little friend live with you?" she says.

"What?"

"The pretty one at the bus station. I think he likes you very much, yes?"

"What're you saying?"

"Nothing. Just he looks, you know . . . so sweet."

"He's just some guy, we were in the army. Why's he going to be living with me?" He pulls out a Lucky, fumbles, breaks it.

She giggles. "Oh, I don't know. I'm interested in many things, you understand?" She looks up at him, but it is too dark for him to make out her eyes, to read them for hidden messages. She leans her head toward her shoulder. "I just wondered if maybe you might have some room?"

He looks down at her. What is this chamaquita up to? Where was she planning to stay before she met him? He tells himself that it is because she is tired that she asks these ridiculous questions. But when he looks down, her face, so pale in the growing starlight, is that of a tired child. Then it's as if a blurry film whirrs into a sudden and blinding focus. Blanca Rosa has come to him like a flower dropped from an angel's bouquet. At last, his break in this crazy life. Who is he to question fate?

He smiles, stuffs the pack of Luckys back into the roll of his T-shirt sleeve, holds out his hand to Blanca Rosa. "Don't worry for nothing, Blanquita. I will take care of you."

Later in the cab of the pickup, he reaches out and strokes Blanca Rosa's cheek. "Do you believe prayers can be answered?" he asks, but he has turned the key of the ignition and doesn't hear her answer over the roar of the engine. It doesn't matter, he looks at her and knows they are. Six months ago, he returned to Mesquite after receiving his aunt's telegram informing him that he'd better come home if he wanted to see his mother alive. In her final moments, she clasped Cisco's hand in hers, her nails painted an undefinable iridescent shade, and fixed her gaze on a plaster statuette of the Virgin of Guadalupe. "Ay, Virgencita," she pleaded, "save mi hijito, my son." She paused, pressed his hand to her pain-withered lips.

It had been her habit to look away when speaking, avoiding eye contact, often causing the other person to turn to see if she was talking to someone else. But as she lay dying, she suddenly stared directly into his eyes, for only a few seconds, but long enough for him to see an expression that he could not describe. He only knew that her gaze made him feel as if he had never known her. Her eyelids quickly shut like blinders before she continued, "He's a good man in his heart. But he's just a man, you know how they are. Please, Virgencita, now he's twenty-eight, send him a decent woman."

As he remembers his mother's prayer, he drives slowly down Main Street and thinks about where to take Blanca Rosa. Of course—how obvious—there is only one place for her. He lowers his boot on the gas pedal and guns the motor with virtuous resolve. Blanca Rosa straightens, rolls down the window, and peers into the darkness of the encroaching desert.

"Don't be afraid, you're safe," he says. He tries to pat her head, but she ducks.

"I'm never afraid," she says. The wind blows into the cab, pulls loose hairs free from her ponytail, and whips them around her face. She returns his stare as boldly as a cat who has never been kicked.

He turns his eyes back to the road. "You were traveling a long time?" Out of his peripheral vision, he sees her glance at him, but he keeps his eyes straight ahead.

"Oh, long enough."

"And your destination was Mesquite? But if you have no family here . . ."

"The truth? I thought you were my destination. I fell asleep during the ride, didn't even know where I was. Then I looked out the window and there was your tattoo. I don't know, I can't explain. I wanted to know you."

"Forget the tattoo." Then softer, "Know where I'm taking you? My mother's house. I never took no woman there before." Blanca Rosa rests her head against the seat and closes her eyes.

He stops at the Last Stop Mart for breakfast food, then fifteen minutes later, he turns off the highway onto the dirt road that leads to an adobe house: a pale blur huddled down in the middle of two acres of fenced desert. "My father built this house with his own hands for my mother," he says once they are in his mother's bedroom. "So at least after he died, she always had her own place. I come out to check things, but this is the first time I'm staying here since she died." He sets the suitcase on the throw rug—a patch of crimson at the foot of the bed—and glances around, tries to see the room from a woman's view.

"My mother always complained about the dust out here, said it was choking her or something." He runs his finger around a vase of plastic orchids on an end table. "She dusted twice, sometimes three times a day."

"So many sorrows," Blanca Rosa says and looks at the melted candles still clustered around a plaster Virgin on the dresser top. She eases down onto the edge of the bed and studies the line his finger has traced through the dust. "Pobrecita, poor thing, how lonely she must have been."

"Even when she was alone in this house, she was never lonely. Always busy, never stopping," he says. Blanca Rosa gazes at him as if she expects him to say more, so he adds, "My mother was a simple woman."

Blanca Rosa smiles in a way that makes him feel stupid. "Oh," she says. Then she adds that she needs a shower and yawns behind her hand, so he points out the bath and wishes her a good sleep. He makes it clear that he will not bother her privacy.

After midnight, he shuffles out of the stifling air of his boyhood bedroom, carries sheet and pillow to the living room. He lies on the sofa, its plastic cover slippery even beneath the sheet, and watches the softly billowing curtain at the open window. Tomorrow he will see about someone coming out to stay with her. In the meantime he will have to be strong so he can control his desire for Blanca Rosa. The idea of having to wait excites him, starts his blood throbbing beneath the jeans that he has kept on to signal his respectful intentions.

A sigh slips from the dark hallway. He jerks into a sitting position and peers toward the shadowy form drifting toward him.

"Come and sleep with me, yes?" she whispers.

"Go back to bed." His voice is thick.

"But the coyotes, they keep howling." Blanca Rosa crosses her arms and rubs them as if she were cold. When she takes a step closer, the heat of her body carries its scent to him: the clean smell of Palmolive soap, the soap his mother used.

Desire prickles his skin. This isn't what he wants, not

yet. But she brushes her hip against his cheek and he knows she has won. When he tries to lower her to him, she resists. "Come with me," she says and pulls him toward his mother's bedroom.

Dawn has just begun to illuminate the night when he eases his cramped body inches away from Blanca Rosa. With feigned hope he searches the sheet for a dark stain. For a moment, he thinks that his fascination for Blanca Rosa has ended, but no, some secret core beckons, somehow even stronger than before. "I forgive you, my adored rosebud," he whispers, for he believes that he should reassure her.

Her cheek expands against his chest when she smiles. Her voice drowsy, she mumbles, "Yes, in my head there are rosebuds, rosebuds and maggots."

He doesn't know what to answer, so he kisses her damp forehead and tells her to wait at the house for him until he gets off work. "Sleep, mi alma," he whispers in her ear, "my soul, you are my soul."

Minutes later, he rolls up chorizo scrambled with eggs in a flour tortilla and bites into the soft taco as he heads out. When he closes the house door behind him, the early-morning sun pours into the screened porch, and for the first time since he has been coming out to oversee the house, he notices the dead geraniums in clay pots on a ledge. He crouches down next a wooden half-barrel beneath the ledge, crumbles the still-fragrant, dried leaves of the hierba buena between his fingers, and remembers the childhood tea his mother used to prepare to soothe his discomfort.

Later, in the back parking lot of Sanchez Brothers Painting, he and two other painters load the truck before starting out downtown to the new office building that is their work site. At first the only noise is the slurping of coffee from thermos cups, then crude jokes are added as the men slowly wake up. When silence returns, he almost tells them about meeting Blanca Rosa, how he plans to marry her. But somehow it doesn't seem like the right time.

As he paints, images of his future run through his head like a filmstrip in brighter-than-life Technicolor. He will have to open a savings account and make plans to control the future so he can become the responsible, dependable man others have always told him he should be. And Blanca Rosa will be the woman his mother became. Suddenly he is tired. He concentrates on the monotonous strokes of his brush.

They are breaking for lunch, climbing into the truck to head out for the El Rancho Drive-In Restaurant, when Paquito walk-runs up the sidewalk, whistles, calls out for Cisco to stop. After telling the other painters that he will catch up with them, Cisco massages the stressed-bunched muscles at the back of his neck, waits for his friend.

At Cisco's side, Paquito holds out his hand for a Lucky, lifts it for Cisco to light off his match. "Some vato's asking questions about that woman, come all the way from Las Vegas."

"And what?" He tries to keep his voice indifferent.

"Says he's her brother." Paquito pauses, exhales the cigarette smoke, a slow stream drifting from his nostrils. "And this *brother*—a very old brother—says she's loquita. His words, man," he adds quickly. "Says he's raising her by hisself and he's got to keep her locked up, you know, because she thinks she can do anything she wants, like she's a man or something."

"And where is this vato now?"

"In town, still looking." Paquito laughs. "Where you going, man?" His voice nips at Cisco's back. "If you're going back to your mother's house, pues, ain't nobody there. You didn't know? That woman left on the bus this morning. But don't think I told that cabrón—I didn't tell him nothing. Me and you, we're like brothers. Ain't that right, carnal?"

"Oye," Paquito calls out when Cisco continues walking away from him, "does she wear some kind of shit on her ankle? That guy—you should've seen him, crying like a woman—he was describing her and says he give her this thing, and she wears it like some kinda sign that she's gonna be good and not run away no more."

Cisco returns to the house alone. In the bedroom the imprint of Blanca Rosa's head remains on his mother's death pillow. He lies down, head sinking into the shallow impression, and when he turns toward the end table, he notices that the streak his finger cleaned through the dust last night is already refilling with the fine particles. The faint scent of sex and Palmolive soap drifts up from the rumpled sheets.

When he runs his hand through the folds, his fingers discover and curl around the anklet. He squeezes it and feels it break between the callouses of his palm. Behind his closed eyelids, he sees the image of Blanca Rosa in the cab of his pickup, her gaze proud behind the wind-freed hair. He smiles.

gloves of her Own

JOSIE STANDS WITH HER FEET firm-flat on the ground, the earth still cool from the desert's night air. With knees braced, she waits for Nana, her grandmother, to finish her mumbled conversation with the dead. Nana had insisted she could not wait for the usual Sunday visit after Mass, had to speak with her husband now. Today, as with all the other visits to the grave site, Josie thinks not of Tata but of her own mother. She glances toward the horizon. "Soon it will be sunrise," Josie says, so that Nana will understand it's time to move on.

Nana shifts her weight from one knee to the other, and as she leans her shoulder against Josie for support, Josie hears a rustling sigh, the silk of Nana's sleeve brushing across her bare calf. Nana lifts her hand to the headstone and says, "Finally, I accept that he is not returning home at the end of the day. But what I can't believe is that I'm still living six weeks after he has gone to his eternal rest." Her voice lowers to a murmur, respectful of the dead. "You see, I thought I was a faithful wife."

"You gave him everything, we both did, what else can we do?" Josie says, but Nana doesn't respond, remains kneeling at the graveside, the skirt of her widow's dress gathering dust.

Josie looks away from the bent head and rounded back covered with a black lace mantilla, watches the orange glow radiating from the distant hill, waits for the slice of red to cut through the earth. When it does, she averts her eyes from the glare. Yards beyond the border of the cemetery, a towering saguaro cactus stretches to the Arizona sky. It looks indifferent now, but later in the afternoon it will cast a shadow. The black column with its arms curved upward toward heaven will stretch, reach its cooling darkness across the empty space to the right of Tata, creep across and beyond his grave.

Nana reaches up one trembling hand and Josie takes it, wraps her other arm around her grandmother and gently lifts. Her palm rests against Nana's ribs, and from beneath the lightness of those bones, she feels the steady beat of Nana's pulse. If she curled her fingers, she could capture the small heart in her hand.

"Look," Nana says and points to the left side of Tata's grave. "My resting place." She points to the other side. "For you. No?" A slight pause, then: "But it wasn't always for you." She clears her throat with a harsh sound, scraping rust from forgotten metal. "We bought these plots soon after your mother was born. I was already forty then, we had given up on having children. You see," she says and stares at the piece of ground, "at one time, he thought she would be with him forever."

"I see," Josie says. Her breathing slows down, shallow so she doesn't miss a word. For as long as she can remember Tata has forbidden any discussion of her mother.

"Maybe," Nana says, "now that Tata is gone . . . maybe you might want to find her?" Nana's eyes slide to the headstone, and she presses her lips together, zips her trembling fingers across them.

"My *dead* mother, Nana?" Josie says this even though long ago she realized her mother hadn't really died, as she had been told. When she entered school, she pasted together enough playground gossip to understand that her mother was dead only by Tata's proclamation. Even so, all these years, the three of them had silently agreed to live the lie. She glances at Tata's grave, almost feels a draft of cool air rising through the concrete slab, vapor curling around her ankles, drawing her to him, reminding her of his repeated advice: *Have no illusions and you'll never be disillusioned.* "I never think about her anymore," Josie says.

Nana makes little *tsking* noises with her tongue. "Don't play games with this old woman. The truth about your mother was always hiding in your eyes. You would like to find her, wouldn't you?"

As a small girl, Josie would have had no problem with Nana's question; she would have answered yes. Back then she lay awake nights and stared out her open bedroom window at the starlit heavens, formed an image of her mother's face in the far-off constellations. But with the years, she learned to tell herself that she had to let go of her illusions. The star she had pretended was her mother exploded into flashes of night glitter, pinpoints of bright light streaming through the darkness, falling to earth, burning out, dust swirling away with the desert's wind.

But when she is alone and honest with her thoughts, she admits to herself that the memory of Margarita remains, an ember, small and glowing deep within. During working hours at the Mesquite Bus Depot, she still searches the eyes of each woman stepping off the Greyhound bus, hopes to glimpse some connection, some shadowed light in the stranger's eye that would blink her mother's name.

Nana links her hand through the crook of Josie's arm and presses, so that they both turn away from the grave and face the car. They start down the path, arms linked, their heels dig-crunching into the gravel, but feet out of step.

"Margarita." Nana pauses and smiles, as if pleased that she has not lost the ability to pronounce that word. "Margarita, Daisy, like the flower. It suited her: bright, alive, never quiet. Not like you and your grandfather. Always chattering, she was." She works the tips of her fingers and thumb against each other like a hand puppet's mouth. "Talk, talk, talk. The house was alive when she was here. Tata couldn't control that one." She looks up at Josie and squints. "Maybe she's still just the same, maybe life has not destroyed her dreams." One corner of her mouth quivers. "What do you think? She's changed?"

"Changed?" Josie wants to laugh but doesn't. "How can I know, Nana? I don't remember how she was, or even how she looked. Tata destroyed all the pictures of her when I was just a baby. Anyway, all that was a long time ago. Better to forget the past."

"You're young, easy for you to say forget." She taps her fingertips, butterfly wings trembling against Josie's inner arm. "My mind has nothing left but memories," Nana says. "And now even they are only ghosts, shadows. Long shadows, longer every year." When Nana turns away from Josie, the mantilla slides off her head, drops to her shoulders, and Josie sees the pale scalp beneath the thinning gray hair.

She drapes one arm around Nana's shoulder, cups her elbow with her free hand, gently nudges forward until Nana resumes her steps and moves on to the Studebaker, Tata's car. Only he drove when they all went out together. Now Josie drives.

Once Nana settles on the passenger side of the sarape-covered front seat, her body rolls into itself like a small armadillo and her eyes squeeze shut, upper and lower lids compressed into a mass of wrinkled folds. She unclasps her black purse, pulls out her rosary beads. There will be no more conversation now. The hum of prayers—their protection from death on the highway—begins. She is Nana once more, the Nana to whom Josie is accustomed: a rounded figure who roams, muttering to herself, from room to room in their house on Frontera Street, searching, searching for who knows what. Since Tata's death, the mumbling has increased and the soles of her house slippers shuffle more insistently across the worn linoleumed floors, *shh-slide, shh-slide,* as sharply quiet as a whisper in the dark.

Thirty minutes later, Josie sits in her chair at their kitchen table, and Nana stands at the stove, pours boiled coffee through a cloth strainer from one saucepan into another. "Your grandfather insisted on having his coffee made like this. The old ways are best, he used to say. And he's always right, isn't he? A wise man, not like me, what do I know?" As Nana talks, she picks up a bag of sugar and directs a white stream into the pan with one hand and stirs with the other. Her voice becomes almost inaudible, talking to herself. "The old ways. That's why he killed her off with his words. Well, she wouldn't obey, would she? She had to be disowned. That's what happens to girls who bring dishonor to their families, isn't it? I imagine you know all about what happened to my Margarita, even if we didn't talk about it in this house."

Nana fills two enameled metal mugs and sets them on the table. She eases down onto the chair across from Josie and lifts a teaspoon of the sweetened-to-syrup coffee to her mouth. Her hand trembles so much, the coffee, like a small river of brown tears, dribbles down her chin. She swipes at it, and while her hand still obscures her mouth, she says, "Tata keeps a secret in a box, a locked metal box."

"Ay, Nana, I don't understand what you're saying. Boxes, secrets, suddenly you are talking about Margarita."

"I have never stopped talking about her. If someone cuts out a piece of my heart, I bleed. Why not? It's only that in this house nobody hears, nobody listens." Nana stirs her coffee round and round, stares at the vapor escaping from the whirlpool of dark liquid. She looks up, her eyes directed at Josie's face, but her gaze unfocused. "Maybe there are letters. What do you think? Could there be letters in that box? You know, only your Tata picked up the mail from the post office. So I say to myself, maybe Margarita writes, but he says nothing. Maybe a return address? You know how he doesn't like to talk. Me, I talk too much, that's my problem, always I was like that, talking but saying nothing, that's my problem—who listens?" Her voice begins to drift away with her gaze.

Josie reaches across the table, gently strokes Nana's forearm. "Nanita," she says, "don't allow yourself these illusions. Tata was not a man to save letters, especially not from her. All that was over for him. You know he never even spoke of her."

"What a child you still are, niña. Tata seldom spoke of anything, do you really believe that means his head, his heart were empty? Who can say what a silent man thinks? Many times I have seen him go to that box, but he closes the bedroom door behind him when I look." She wags her finger. "He can't shut the door fast enough. I know what's what in this house. It's in the closet, on the top shelf, pushed to the back. He doesn't like anyone to touch his things, and he is the man of the house. But now, pues, he's gone. We don't have to obey the dead, do we? I asked his permission today, but he doesn't answer. Maybe it's a good sign?"

Without waiting for a response, Nana says, "I can't reach—my arthritis—but if you stand on a chair, well, there's no problem. I cannot find her without your help." Nana stands, hobbles on feet swollen from unaccustomed dress shoes toward the arched doorway of the bedroom she shared with Tata for all the years of their marriage.

Still sitting, Josie yawns, clasps her hands, cracks her knuckles, stretches her arms above her head until she almost lifts herself from the hard-back chair Tata made for her years ago, when she first learned to sit by herself. Her behind fits comfortably into the scoop it has worn into the woven seat, and she cannot bring herself to leave it yet.

Nana looks back over her shoulder. "You're not coming?"

Josie glances at her wristwatch to avoid Nana's eyes. "I have to clean the chicken coop before I go to work," she says. It is true, after all. Tata used to handle all the outside housework, while Josie supplemented his small pension with her grill job at the Mesquite Bus Depot snack shop. Now her duties have increased.

"It will only take a few minutes," Nana says. "Later you can clean, no?"

Josie pushes her palms against the tabletop edge, oil-cloth sticky on her skin, scoots the chair back and stands. She decides to help Nana although she's certain the contents of the box will disappoint her grandmother. There will only be documents, receipts, dry official papers of recorded facts. Nana is wrong about Tata's thoughts; he was practical, not sentimental. Josie knew him better than anyone, and she has learned his life's lessons almost as if they were her own.

Nana moves aside when Josie carries her chair from the kitchen and sets it in front of the closet. "Up there,"

Nana says and points to the long wooden shelf above the rack of Tata's clothes, blue Western shirts and earth-stained jeans hanging on wire hangers.

Josie climbs onto the chair, and balancing against the door frame, pushes herself onto her tiptoes. Only the top edge of the gray metal box is visible. "I'll need a stick," she says and looks down at Nana.

"Yes, yes," Nana says. She returns with the broom and something more. "Here," she says and holds up one of Tata's work gloves. "To protect your hands. Once, when I was just a girl, I was stung by a scorpion—I reached into a place where I couldn't see and, *ayyyy,*" she moans, as if the pain were still with her. She begins to mutter to herself and Josie hears only scattered words about cutting the sting, sucking out the poison before it's too late, and other words she can't make out, so she stops listening.

Josie slides her right hand into the glove. Time has molded the leather to Tata's hand. The thumb's length suits her, but still it's too roomy, stretched by the width of his thumb; the first three fingers bend to the right, curved to the angle of his rheumatoid arthritis, but the small finger space—a space that Tata never filled—still holds the generic shape of a new glove. Tata had lost that finger to the misjudged swing of a fellow worker's machete. Josie spreads her fingers, flexes them.

She slides the broom handle back, knocks the box forward, then reaching in with her gloved hand, pulls it out and swipes at the dust before handing it to Nana. "It's pretty light," Josie says to prepare Nana, "so if there *are* letters, there can't be very many."

"The key is in his top dresser drawer," Nana says, but doesn't move from the bed, remains sitting on the edge, her small feet dangling in midair.

Josie slides open the drawer and the silvery key, a tiny star of light, winks at her from a dark corner. She picks it up, and as she turns back to Nana, she gasps. Out of the corner of her eye, she glimpsed a reflection in the mirror. She'd forgotten she wore the glove, and for a second she thought it was Tata's hand, Tata's hand at the end of her arm.

When she lifts the metal lid, a ghost-faint scent of lavender wafts up. Inside the box there are two things: a tortoiseshell hairbrush with a few long strands of black hair tangled through the natural bristles, and beneath, something dark coiled around itself and wrapped in clear plastic. Josie places the brush on Nana's lap. Nana whispers, "Oh, I remember that," clutches the bedspread, rocks back and forth.

Josie lays out the package, unfolds the plastic. With each lifted layer, the scent grows stronger. Finally. A braid of the blackest hair, with a delicate purple ribbon woven through the three strands.

Nana makes small twittering noises, rubs her fists into her closed eyes, opens them again. "Is this an old lady's mirage, or can it be true?" she says, "Tata said he destroyed it."

Josie lifts the braid, silky and resilient as though it breathed life. She grasps its thickest end, held together by a rubber band, places it in one of Nana's uplifted palms, stretches it out and across to Nana's other hand. At the tapered end, the curls have been brushed into one springy swirl, slips of purple ribbon peeking through the black.

"I always added lavender water to her rinse," Nana says. "Purple was her favorite color, you see. Such hair, she could sit on it. He wouldn't allow her to cut it, forbid her to cut it. But she didn't obey." Nana strokes the braid as she speaks. "It happened maybe two weeks before she ran away. She came home late from school one day, walked in carrying her hair in her hand, held it high and away from her like a dead animal. 'My headaches,' she said, 'are finished.'

"He snatched it away from her, said he would burn it with the other trash." Nana sighs, lifts the hair, clutches it to her face, inhales. "After that, nothing was the same. She ran away, only came back two years later to leave you with me. And then gone. Forever? You know, the day she cut it, it didn't have a purple ribbon, and it was not braided. It was Tata who liked it braided."

Nana begins to mumble, first words that Josie can't make out, then louder. "Lies and deception," she says. "Illusions locked in a box are still illusions. Isn't that so?" She holds up one end of the braid. "But that's not enough for us. We will find our Margarita, isn't that so?"

Josie can say nothing; the words won't come. Her head is moving, but she doesn't know if she's nodding it up and down or shaking it from side to side. Her shoulders tremble when she shrugs and turns away. "I have work to do," she says.

When she steps outside, away from the interior of the house and its cooling adobe walls, the blinding sun hits her like a fist. Her eyes squinted, she makes her way to the table and chairs, set up under the shade of a mesquite, the table where she and Tata spent many hours playing dominoes, creating mazes, snakes across the tabletop, matching dots of white on black. Pinpoints of white, stars in the darkness of night.

She shakes her head as if the memories she had thought forgotten could be released from inside her mind and tossed out, scattered out into the air to shrivel in the blinding sun. She opens her eyes and focuses yards away on the chicken coop. Tata's work to be completed. Inside the coop, the chickens cackle, proud of the eggs that Josie has not yet gathered. With the back of her gloved hand, she presses a plump hen aside, closes her free hand around the warm, pebbly surface of the egg, and brings it out. As a child, she used to help Tata gather eggs, both of them working side by side, silently, no words necessary because they understood each other. That is what she believed then.

The hen flies at her, squawking, pecking. Josie stumbles backward out of the coop and back into the sunlight. She grabs at the door to keep from falling, and the glove catches, hooks on the sliding latch. She pulls her hand free.

Josie glances at Tata's glove, still hanging on the hook, the shape of his hand rigid, unchanged. She reaches out to retrieve the glove, stops midway when she hears Nana call her from the kitchen door. "Josie," she says, "we can give her memory life again, I know we can, but you must help me."

Josie's hand drops back to her side. She can afford to buy gloves of her own. She turns, walks toward Nana's hope-filled voice.

butterfly

DONALD MURRAY KNOWS HE should force his gaze to drift about his fifth-grade classroom, make certain the children aren't cheating on the pop history quiz, but his stare stays wrapped around his newest student, Tonantzin Salazar. She sits in her assigned seat close to him. With her near, he can almost forget the smells of child-bitter sweat and the corn-chip odor of dirty socks that permeate the hot room. Sometimes he thinks that smell will suffocate him.

His gaze creeps over Tonantzin's face, her mouth, her full lips coming together, slowly pulling apart, edges sticking, clinging to each other in the saliva-moist corners. He's never sure if she's praying or just moving her lips while she reads. As he watches her, something dark and thick stirs inside him.

He swallows hard to still his quivering Adam's apple, but he cannot still his hands. The long, pale fingers seem to be separate from him, flutter over the surface of his desk, straighten papers, touch books, pick up then drop paper clips. He grinds the sore soles of his feet onto the pebbles he dropped inside his Hush Puppy loafers this morning. Somewhere, he'd read that it was possible to fool a polygraph machine by placing a sharp object inside one's shoes and then pressing down when answering innocuous questions. Physical reaction to the sudden stab sets off the machine, and its mechanical arm draws erratic lines that don't differentiate between pain and lie. Not that he thinks he would ever be hooked up to such a contraption, no, it's only that it might be a way to scare away his unchaste thoughts.

But the pain isn't deep enough to erase the pictures forming, pushing out from the serpentine recesses of his brain. His eyes dart about the room in search of diversion, skim above the bent heads of those students still struggling over test papers.

He stops at the farthest corner of the classroom, looks directly into the mocking eyes of Riquis Valencia. The boy smirks, slowly sticks out the tip of his tongue, and fake-farts a raspberry, long and loud.

Murray claps his hands to stop the children's laughter, but the wooden floor vibrates with it. He stands up so suddenly, his long legs don't clear the desk. His thighs bang against the edge with enough force to lift one side. When he straightens, he rocks back, presses his full weight onto the pebbles. He winces and does a little hopping step backward.

"Uy, uy, I didn't know you could dance so good, Miss— oh, excuse me—I mean *Mr.* Murray," Riquis shouts over the noise, follows up with a hoot.

Murray glances at Tonantzin, thankful she hasn't joined in the derision. He claps his hands again, swallows the hurt lumping in his throat. He thinks of the two years he has been in Mesquite, how he has worked so diligently with these children, tried to make a difference in their lives— why can't they see how much he cares? "Children, you must learn to behave," he says. "Stop, I say."

Murray folds his arms across his chest, shouts, "Must I go for Mr. Garcia?" Everyone knows about the principal's inch-thick paddle with holes drilled for maximum impact, and how the short, muscular Garcia smiles as he whacks students in the presence of their classmates. Murray doesn't like calling him in, but if the children leave him no choice, he will. After a stray whistle and a halfhearted giggle, the class returns to near silence. He tells them to pass their quizzes forward, lay their heads on their desks, and reflect on how they can be more compassionate to their fellowman.

"That means everyone," he says. Riquis rolls his eyes but does as he is told.

Murray collects the papers from the front of the rows and glances at Tonantzin, slouched, but chin propped up in a cupped palm. He doesn't insist she put her head down along with the others. After all, he knows she isn't one of the troublemakers, and he doesn't believe she's defying him, just didn't hear, that's all. He returns to his seat behind his desk and waits, thankful that he can watch Tonantzin without being watched.

A monarch butterfly drifts through an open window, glides toward her, flutters above her arm, alights on her sleeve. Its wire-thin proboscis probes, tries in vain to sip nectar from the flowers of faded pink woven into the material of her dress. Murray nibbles at the dead skin flaking his chapped lips, can almost taste the sweetness that the butterfly dreams of sucking from the moist depths of the blossoms. Faraway baby-tongue pink.

The lunch bell clangs. He starts, waves at the children to go. All but Tonantzin grab their lunch bags and rush, pushing and shoving, from the room. She stretches her fingers forward, reaches out for the butterfly's shadow as it flies away. After it floats through the window, she slides out of her seat, walks slowly, her movements fluid like sun-warmed honey. She keeps her gaze on the floor as she passes his desk.

"Toni," Murray says, loud enough for only her ears. He repeats her name and interlaces the trembling fingers of his hands, clenches them.

She keeps her head ducked but turns it toward him. "Tonantzin," she says.

"Toni's so much simpler, isn't it?" He tries to chuckle, but the vibration in his throat becomes a cough. For a second, he thinks he sees in Tonantzin that veiled look that often glazes many of the Mexican children's eyes—an expression he finds so hard, so ungrateful—that now his face flushes with irritation. But no, he decides, it's only his imagination: She isn't like the others. Although he never says the words aloud, the truth is they somehow repel him. But for her there is hope. He knew that the day she arrived from Superior, six weeks ago.

"Remember," he says, "I'm coming to visit you and your parents Saturday. Now, that's tomorrow, don't forget." His gaze drops to her slender brown neck, to the chain of silver that she always wears, the two tarnished threads disappearing beneath the scoop of her dress neckline. She lifts her thin shoulders, drops them in a shrug, and something pointy hanging at the end of the chain slides up, down beneath the material of her dress.

"You did take the note home?" he says.

She nods. "Only my father says he can't meet with you, he has to go someplace."

"That's fine, we'll talk to Mom."

"She visits with my grandmother in Superior," she says, turns to walk away. Murray reaches for her wrist, marvels at how delicate her bones feel inside the grip of his hand, as if he could snap them with one sudden twist. He smiles, holds on.

"How long has it been since you've been to church? Be honest, now."

She tugs at her arm, looks toward the door, as if expecting to see someone, but all the children are outside.

"Just as I imagined," he says when she remains silent. "And I would venture to say that you've never been to a Christian church, very different from the Catholics. Oh, you'll love Sunday school and the wonderful stories of Jesus." He'll speak with her parents tomorrow, he says, and tell them that on Sundays he's willing to pick her up for services, starting this week. He hears himself talking too fast, too much, and his mouth is dry. He pauses, looks at her bowed head, and feels he needs to add one more sentence. He pats her arm, says, "He loved little children, too. Jesus, I mean."

When she doesn't respond, Murray releases her arm. "I'll bring a little surprise," he says. "You like surprises, don't you?" He hopes she will want to stay by his desk now, drop her customary reticence, sprinkle him with a fairy dusting of excited questions. She continues toward the door, walks away from him. The outline of her shoulder blades nudge against the back of her dress, small wings, folded, hidden.

An angel, he thinks, his own darling angel.

Once she is out of the room, Murray pulls his metal lunch box from the bottom desk drawer and turns his chair to face the window. He stares out to the box hedge at the side of the building, waits to see if Tonantzin will slip into the space between the hedge and the outside wall, as she sometimes does. When she hides there, he can sit back out of her line of vision, and while munching on potted ham and mayonnaise sandwiches, watch her small face go relaxed and dreamy. Thinking no one sees her, she'll talk to herself, sometimes smiling, sometimes frowning, but always far away.

He imagines her wearing that same expression, sitting next to him in his car while he drives her to services next

Sunday. When she first came to Mesquite, it hadn't immediately occurred to him to invite her to his church. And he can't remember now if, once the idea did come to him, his first thought was to save her soul or to find an excuse for spending more time with her. Surely, he tells himself, it must be the former.

He squints. What's she doing? Instead of going behind the hedge, she stands at the edge of the concrete square that runs the length of the building. He wonders if she has no one to eat with, is about to call out to her when a small boy bursts out the other end of the building. Flaco Valencia, Riquis's younger brother, runs toward her, panting, a wrinkled, brown paper bag clutched to his chest like a football. He reaches her, drops one hand to his side, close to her, his knuckles brushing against hers. They turn their backs to him and run away, side by side, onto the unpaved playground.

In the classroom, Murray cracks his knuckles, one by one.

"Donald, I have been looking for you," a woman's voice calls from the doorway behind him. She is so loud that for a second he feels as if his thoughts have been revealed.

"You startled me," he says to explain his reddening face.

Dolores Durán, the only teacher who has remained friendly to him since he came to Mesquite Elementary from Indiana, *tip-taps* across the floor in her open-toed stiletto heels, red-lacquered toes revealed, tips curling over the ends, grasping. She stands next to him now. He leans his upper body to the side, a few inches away from her. But her smell still nauseates him. It's a strange mixture of flowery perfume and some other unfamiliar sweetish odor that he suspects might be the remains of early-morning sex. That's why he wants to keep his distance from her: He's heard all those stories about her enticing men of all ages into her bed. He hasn't abstained from temptations of the flesh all these years just to have himself defiled by such a woman.

She bends over, looks out the window, and follows the line of his gaze: Tonantzin and Flaco huddle together at the top of the shaded bleachers at the far edge of the field. Flaco reaches into his lunch bag, pulls out something—one of those tortillas with refried beans and chiles, Murray guesses—and tears it in two, hands one piece to Tonantzin.

"He's a good boy," Dolores says and straightens. "You see," she says and smiles at Murray as if she knows what he has been thinking, "now the little girl—your new student, yes?—she has something to eat. The poor always find their own way. You spend too much time worrying about your students."

"I know, I know," Murray says, doesn't admit that it hadn't really registered that Tonantzin had nothing for lunch. "It just appears so hopeless for most of these children," he says, encouraged by Dolores's kind impression of him. "But Toni, well, she's one that could actually make something of herself, and look who she associates with. She needs to be around a more positive influence. Just look at him. He'll never amount to anything, not him or his brother. You know the type, Dolores. Anyone can see what he's after."

"Ay, Donald, they are only babies." She studies him with such narrowed eyes, he knows it's better to say no more. Would a woman such as Dolores be capable of understanding the depth of his feelings for Tonantzin?

He remains silent, stares at her until she feels the need to explain that she stopped by to invite him to join the other teachers in the lounge. They've prepared a surprise birthday cake for the fresh-out-of-college teacher, Margie Whissen.

"Too much work to do," he says, not offering his opinion of Margie, just moving his gaze to the stack of quizzes. Dolores's invitation to join them if he changes his mind wafts back over her shoulder. He nods although he does not intend to start mixing in with that group.

Now and then, though, he does stand outside the closed door of the lounge, where he can listen to what's going on without having to break out into a sweat making small talk. Not that he's so interested, it's only that since the problems at Lincoln School in Indiana—those misunderstandings about the little girls, how before recess, he helped them button up their jackets and sweaters, warned them to cushion their budding breasts. After all, a hit from a playground ball might damage them, prevent them from suckling the babies they would surely have someday. Why was that such a terrible thing to say?

But people twist things to suit them, the way his colleagues had done. It was in the teachers' lounge at Lincoln where the hurtful gossip that lost him his job began. That's why now he makes certain he knows if he's being discussed. Sure enough, one day as he stood, back against the wall, outside the lounge, his breath as quiet as a shadow, he heard Margie Whissen squeeze his name in among her snickers.

It wasn't enough that she turned down his earlier offer of a movie and dinner, no, she had to tell everyone in the lounge about it, imitating his nervously high voice, his stammer when he had asked her out. She went on to say how he reminded her of her home, *ha-ha*. A maple leaf in the fall he looked like, she said: dry spine curving, thin edges curling, a body turning in on itself.

He shifts back to the window, leans on the sill, picks at the peeling paint, and studies Tonantzin's face in profile. Flaco glances up, appears to be looking at him. Murray wonders if he should wave or merely smile, but before he decides, Flaco turns back to Tonantzin, lips to her ear, covers his mouth behind a cupped hand. At this distance, their features are not clearly defined to his weakened sight, and their small brown faces are almost indistinguishable, until Flaco turns back to face him, laughs, throws back his head, mouth open, teeth a flash of white in his dark face. Murray squints, strains to see Tonantzin. She's not laughing, he's certain. But is that a smile?

Murray scrapes his chair back, pulls out the other halved triangle of his sandwich, refuses to think about Tonantzin and Flaco together. He closes his eyes, forces an image of her to fill his mind. But his creation does not wear outdated secondhand store rags that make her look like a midget adult from another era. No, he imagines a more respectable outfit, one like the little girls back home used to wear: angora sweaters in robin's egg blue with a buttoned-on lace collar; full, gathered skirt swirling around fawn-delicate legs; patent leather Mary Jane shoes with ankle socks, bleached to a blinding white. He sees her sitting primly in the polished wood of the front pew of his church. And he's there, too. His arm encircles her, pulls her to him, allows her to lean on him. She needs his help. Who else will save her?

Saturday, mid-morning, Murray's station wagon roars up the paved incline of Frontera Street. When he reaches the top of the steep hill, the asphalt ends suddenly, and he brakes in the crosslike shadow of a utility pole. He hunches down and glances across the front seat, out the right passenger window, squints to read the names on the numerous locked mailboxes nailed to the wooden pole. *Salazar* #363$\frac{1}{2}$, and next to it, *Valencia*.

He tightens his bolo tie with one hand, reaches down next to his side, pats the white Bible—new back still unbroken, dedication to Tonantzin carefully penned inside in iris-scented, lavender ink. When he noses the car over the crest, begins the descent to her apartment, the Bible slides to the edge of the seat. He grabs at it, wedges it between his thighs. Until his little conversation with Tonantzin yesterday, this was to be the only surprise. But after Dolores's observations, he decided to add a little something, treats in the Safeway grocery bag on the floor of the car.

He rides the brake as he edges down the hill, presses lightly on the pedal. Last night he removed the pebbles from his shoes, but his feet still ache. He wishes he had rolled up the windows, feels vulnerable, unprotected. From what, he's not certain. It's only that he's never been in this area before, and it seems even more foreign than the rest of the town.

He's accustomed to the tall chain-link fence that separates Mesquite into two cities. He has crossed over a few times to visit the odd curio store or restaurant in Mexico, but always at the crossing near downtown, where uniformed immigration officials keep the perimeters well-defined.

And at that crossing there are businesses facing both sides, giving him a sense of purpose, of importance; here the fence cuts through a residential section, leaves him somehow uncomfortable, uncertain of what is expected of him. On the other side of the fence, a group of ragged boys bunch up on the sidewalk. They notice his car, his gaze, and begin to yell at him in Spanish, make obscene gestures with their hands and fingers.

He quickly turns his head away from them, to the window on his other side. He has already passed one house, its squat exterior hiding behind overgrown pomegranate bushes. Beyond, there is only sage, dry grass, and mesquite trees until he nears the bottom of the decline and a small adobe house. A bent old woman, dressed in black, stands by a rosebush in the front yard, seems to be studying it for bugs or disease. As he nears, she peers at him beneath the shade of her straw hat, quickly turns, scuttles back into her house as if he were a hawk swooping down on her.

Yards beyond, at the foot of the hill, the apartment building, a two-story redbrick, stares back at him as blankly as a blind eye. Three mesquite trees in the side yard form a triangle, and from the branch of one, a small boy hangs upside down, his hands circled around his eyes, as if he were pretending to be looking through binoculars. Murray follows the aim of the binoculars to the top of a hill behind the apartments, sees only houses.

As Murray's station wagon nears, the boy twists, stares at him through rolled hands: Flaco Valencia. After Murray edges his car up the road, stops next to the trunk of the tree, engine idling, Flaco flips off the branch.

Murray smiles, wonders which popular cowboy Flaco imagines himself to be. "Are you on the lookout for Indians?" he asks.

"Nah, I got to watch out for the bad guys." Flaco returns Murray's smile, but Murray feels the bite in the flint black of his eyes.

"Well, then," Murray says, explains he's looking for Toni Salazar's apartment but doesn't see any numbers. "Is this the one?" he says and points to the door on the side of the building. "She said it was downstairs."

"No, Joaquín lives here," the boy says as if Murray should know or care who that is.

Murray taps his fingers on the leather-covered steering wheel. When Flaco goes silent, stares at him, Murray tries to summon up his teacher's voice-of-authority tone. But, out of his classroom, in these strange surroundings, his voice takes on a tinny sound, *ti-tank, ti-tank,* like beating on a child's toy drum. "Come along now," he says. "Toni and her father are expecting me."

"Toni?" Flaco says, stubs the toe of his shoe in the dirt, as if considering this. "You must be too late," he finally says, "because her father left. He's a famous boxer, Kid Salazar. You never hear about him?"

Murray shakes his head, tells him he doesn't follow the sport. He dabs beneath his chin with his forearm, stops the sweat from dripping. "I have something for her," he says.

Flaco looks in the car, drops his eyes to the Bible still locked between Murray's thighs. "You gonna read the Bible today, even when it ain't Sunday? Anyway, you can't go in her house when her father's gone. Don't look so good."

"Oh, come now, it's only me," Murray says, then adds, "Any day is the right day for the Word." When Flaco only stares at him, Murray shifts the car back in gear, tells the boy he doesn't need his assistance. He eases off the brake, allows the car to roll forward.

Flaco stretches out his arm, points it to show a curve around the building. "Around the other side, that's where they live."

Murray glances in the rearview mirror when he pulls away. Flaco walks behind, a small figure almost lost in the clouds of dust spitting out behind the tires. When Murray reaches the other side of the building, he sees her, forgets about Flaco.

Tonantzin sits cross-legged, her back against a rotting log in the dirt yard of her apartment, her skirt scoop-draped between her knees. He catches a glimpse of blue panties, and deep inside his throat, a small, quivering moan escapes. He waves, wants to call out but is afraid his voice will quaver.

She continues to stare at the ground for a second, then

her hand away.

es. "She can take it, pain don't bother her."

walks a few feet away, out of Flaco's and
lows, gently places the freed butterfly onto a
ock.

palms have begun to itch. He scratches one,
. "It won't survive," he says.

if it don't?" Flaco says, stares up at him.

ifts his weight, clears his throat. "Toni?" he
s question mark but is not certain what the
e refuses to look at him. It doesn't matter. He
ow that he was wrong about her, she is just
them. There's no saving her. He turns, walks
ldren's laughter skitters across the ground
his spine. He is suddenly aware, once more,
g in the soles of his feet.

looks at him from beneath her bangs, her gaze still unfocused, still lost somewhere in her private world. He reaches for the Bible and Safeway bag, slides out of the car. Her eyes move, look around him, beyond. Murray turns.

Flaco stands, his legs akimbo, at the edge of the dirt yard. He hooks his thumbs in his jeans and hitches them up before walking over to them. "She don't have time for too much talk," he says and glances at the sun. "In a little minute we're going to the house of this guy I know. He's got baby cats. We're getting one for her, a special one."

"Toni can speak for herself," Murray says.

Flaco shrugs. "She don't like to talk so much. More, she likes to think, all the time she's thinking. So I talk. What you got in that bag?"

Murray ignores the question, clutches his gifts to his chest, eases down onto the log, his knees bent at sharp angles. Murray follows her gaze to the ground in front of her. An army of fire ants hold captive a butterfly. Thorn-sharp pincers have sunk into one black and orange wing, but the other flutters free, gossamer, trembling, pointing toward heaven.

"A penny for your thoughts," Murray whispers.

"A penny ain't nothing," Flaco says.

"It's just an expression," Murray says. "I would like to know what Toni is thinking."

"Nothing, just about things," she mumbles. She hesitates, adds, "Papi says no visitors."

"Oh, but I'm not a stranger, I'm your teacher." Murray squeezes the bundle at his chest harder, his large knuckles straining yellow-white beneath his pink skin. If only he could reach down, smooth her hair, so tousled, wanton looking.

She lifts her head to glance up at him, and when she does, her too-large blouse tepees out on one side, reveals a tiny nipple, a whisper in pinkish brown. He can't believe she isn't aware of what she's doing—intentionally tempting him? He bites his lip so hard, he fears he's cut it, dabs at it with two fingers, but there's no blood.

"What's that on the end of your chain?" Murray says, tries to relax the tightness in his throat.

He looks up when Flaco's shadow shades his face. "It's la Virgen de Guadalupe," Flaco says. "Also a chuparosa, you know, one of them little birds that look like big butterflies, what do you call? A hummingbird, yeah."

Murray chuckles, refuses to make eye contact with Flaco, looks back at the top of Tonantzin's head. "Now, why would you be wearing a hummingbird? Hmmm," he hums and hopes she'll smile. "Is that your favorite bird?"

"My grandmother gave it to me," she says, her voice serious. "It's an Aztec warrior. Died and came back like a hummingbird."

"Oh, that's a fun story, but that's all it is, you know that, don't you, honey?" Murray pats her head, doesn't allow his hand to slide down the strands of hair. "But now wearing the other, well, that's one of the things we'll talk about at Sunday school, you'll learn about false idols. You do want to go to heaven someday, don't you?"

"Your peoples—over there where you come from—they don't need no salvation?" Flaco says.

Murray closes his eyes for a second, takes a deep breath, blows out a sigh. "Well, then," he says, "let's see what's in the bag." He sets it next to Tonantzin. When she doesn't open it, Murray reaches down, impatient, pulls out a box of Moon Pies and a package of strawberry Kool-Aid.

"See? What do you say you go inside and make up a nice pitcher, just like on the package," he says. "We can drink it out here."

Tonantzin says nothing.

"You got sugar in t
"Sugar? Why, no."
each other, understan
Kool-Aid, Toni?"

She shakes her he
"Well, no matter,
it's her false pride th
"It's okay if you don't
with me."

"She didn't say s
way, we don't like no
They both stare at h

For a second, b
black and hard as F
the box of sweets,
can't lift the flap nea
to Tonantzin.

She stares at th
reaches forward, fin
pers to her in Spa
Flaco says, "We like
make some today."

Murray holds t
accept his offering
behind her, remair
follow. Like partne
ants continue to i
a distant anthill. T
fly and ants into
thumb and forefin
the ants. One sinl
her skin.

Murray stand
he says.

She jerks
Flaco smi
Tonantzin
Murray's sha
sun-warmed r
Murray's
then the othe
"And wha
Murray sh
says, hears hi
question is. Sh
understands n
like the rest of
away. The chi
behind him, up
of the throbbin

hotel arco iris

DOLORES DURÁN ROLLS HER still-narrow hips into an
overstuffed easy chair and ignores the two sharp raps at
her front door. She recognizes the knock: Mercy, her friend
and washerwoman, has come to pick up the week's dirty
laundry. These days it's difficult for Dolores to look at
Mercy without squirming, wondering if she knows about
Carlos. Well, Dolores figures, that's probably finished anyway; he hardly ever calls anymore, not even to ask what
new gift she has bought him this time. And after all,
what does Mercy have to worry about? She has three children and another one coming, and she's still young, at least
ten years younger than Dolores. Although she doesn't
look it, Dolores thinks, and pats her hair, freshly hennaed
yesterday.

She listens to Mercy's heaving breathing on the other
side of the door, and quietly stretches her arm in front of
her, turns it to the sunlight streaming through the open
space between the living room drapes. Her newest bangle
sparkles, a wide circle of 14-karat gold, pushed midway up
her forearm behind the rest of her to-the-wrist collection of
gold bracelets. She's been buying one for herself every
month since last year's Mother's Day. That was the seven-
teenth year of helping her fourth-grade students make

cards of pink construction paper and red-penciled hearts for their mothers. And almost as many years of listening to some of the other teachers at Mesquite Elementary School brag, in the teachers' lounge, about the gifts they received from their own children at home. She spins a bracelet at her wrist. Anyway, she's better off; her lifestyle keeps her free, young. Spin, spin. Let them listen to her boast for a change.

Mercy knocks again, louder now. Doesn't she ever give up? So afraid of losing her husband, whining to Dolores, begging her to tell her if she knows anything. Dolores isn't sure if Mercy really doesn't know what's been going on or if she's just afraid to be open. With Mercy's new baby coming, she can't afford to lose the extra money that Dolores's soiled clothes bring, or the recommendations that Dolores has promised to give to the other teachers.

With the tip of her fingernail, manicured in what Perlita at the beauty salon proclaimed polish of the week, Tropicana Orange, Dolores lifts the bracelet now, slides it slowly around her arm, feels the machine-smooth coolness against her too-warm flesh. Her nails trail higher, over each bangle, onto her bare skin, higher, feathery circles on the pale blue veins in the crook of her elbow, drag lightly up the silkiness of her inner arm. She shivers. Her half-closed eyes don't move from the first bracelet, the outer surface of gold, etched designs of bamboo, glitter of cut edges. With painful slowness, her gaze moves to the end table at her side, the pink telephone. It is still silent, as silent as the rest of her childless and husbandless home.

Mercy rattles the screen door and Dolores wishes she had never become friends with her in the first place. Last year Mercy's son Riquis was one of her students, so when Dolores ran into the family one night at a local park, Riquis introduced her to his parents. As she spoke with Mercy, who was apologizing for not making it to the last parent-teacher meeting and explaining that the baby had been ill, Carlos stood behind his wife. His gaze, hotter than the day's sun, melted a path down Dolores's body, paused at her breasts, lingered longer at her hips. She was shocked that he would do this with his wife standing there, even if it was out of her range of vision; still, her thoughts grew moist and warm beneath his gaze. He didn't call right away; it wasn't until later, after she and Mercy became friends, that things developed.

Mercy rattles the screen door so hard, Dolores thinks it might come off its hinges. "Isn't that you in there, Dolores?" Mercy calls.

Dolores glances up and sees Mercy's outline, eyes hand-shaded, nose pressed against the window, glass breath-steamed. "It's me, your friend Mercy."

Dolores nods, slides her hands to the edge of the arm-rests, presses on cabbage roses of faded scarlet, and stands up. When she opens the door, she returns Mercy's hug and says, "Sorry, I was lost in thought and didn't hear you," but pulls away when Mercy's pregnancy-swollen stomach pushes against her. Was that a tiny kick she felt?

Dolores turns and leads Mercy to the kitchen, starts a stream of words so thick and fast, Mercy can't interrupt. The coffee, Dolores says, is still hot, and she has some sweet bread that she bought yesterday across the line in Mexico, and she can't chat too long today because she has so many papers to grade because a teacher works even on Sundays, but she doesn't really mind all the work because, after all, hasn't it bought her all this. She waves her ban-gled arm to take in the expanse of her home.

"Yes, yes, you're very lucky," Mercy says and follows into the kitchen. She eases her bloated body onto a kitch-enette chair, the vinyl-covered seat whooshing with her weight, and groans.

"Luck has nothing to do with it, my friend," Dolores says, ignores the groan that was much too loud and prolonged to be real. "Planning and hard work, that's what it takes," she continues. "Some women choose to put their future in the hands of a man. Me? I have always taken care of myself. This is all one needs in life." She rubs her thumb against her first two fingers to signal money.

"Yes, a paycheck changes things," Mercy says. "Me, I have nothing, no job, no money." She glances at the two pillowcases full of dirty laundry propped against a kitchen cabinet. "Not that you don't pay me a fair price, no, no, I mean only that it doesn't pay enough to support me and my children. If I lose Carlitos, what will happen to me, Dolores? What will happen to me and my children?"

Dolores shakes her head slowly and stirs two teaspoonsful of sugar into her bitter coffee. She looks away, out her kitchen window to the backyard garden: a garden of weeds, saplings from windblown seeds of unknown origins, seeds blown across the Sonoran desert to take root in her yard. She waters her garden during the yearly drought season, even though it is forbidden, fills the concrete birdbath, mushrooming out of the tangle of weeds, sits back to watch the bright rainbow that forms over the basin. She wishes there were a rainbow now.

"Ay, Dolores, you must go see this curandera," says Mercy, spews the words out so suddenly and with such force, her spit sprays across the table, an arc of saliva over the plate of bread between them.

Dolores frowns at the shift in conversation; this is not the first time Mercy has mentioned curanderas. "And why must I see a healer? I'm not sick," she says.

"I know that you're an educated woman—not ignorant like me," Mercy says. "But I tell you this one, well, she's not really a healer, she is a specialist, an adviser in matters of the heart. She can see you better than you see yourself, help you find what you are looking for." Mercy doesn't look at Dolores while she speaks; instead she studies the bread, as if choosing just the right piece were of great importance to her.

"Find love, you mean?" Dolores says, although she is not certain what she is looking for.

"Only last week I was visiting Doña Refugio, this specialist of the heart, and I mentioned you."

"Charlatans, all of them."

"Ay Mujer, I myself have used her professional services because of my little problem with Carlitos—there is no other like her."

"She probably lives too far," Dolores says.

"Not far for you, you have a car," Mercy says. "You can drive most of the way. She lives on the Mexican side—you cross the border downtown at Frontera Street, continue parallel to Frontera, all the way down to where the sidewalk ends, then you walk the rest of the way up the hill."

She pats her stomach and adds, "I have her, Doña Refugio, to thank for this. A packet of her powders in my man's hot chocolate every night—without telling him, naturally— and *poof*. Oh, sometimes he comes home late, like all men, but no more gone all night, you understand." She twists her wedding band, too tight on her swollen fingers.

Dolores picks at the label on a can of Carnation milk, shreds the paper into a neat pile in the center of the table. When Carlos used to crawl into her bed—sheets as cool and lonely as a desert night—he filled her head with his words of love and her body with his heat. A heat that she craves, for her blood has begun to creep cold through her veins and she feels a chill deep inside where the fever of her flesh does not reach. While she felt the sure beat of his heart next to hers, she wanted Mercy to find out, but now, well, Carlos's heartbeat has grown faint with distance and Mercy pleads silently with eyes shadowed by pain. "She didn't say for sure another woman?" Dolores says in what she hopes is a very casual tone.

"What she didn't see was the other woman's name, couldn't make out the letters." Mercy picks up the fan that's wedged between her belly and her thighs. *Swish, swish,* goes the cardboard that advertises Orozco's Funeral Home (*We Respect Love of Friends and Family—Entrust Your Dead to Us, Fair Prices Guaranteed*). "If only I knew for sure," Mercy says. "I'd pull out her hairs, the ones down there, one by one, that's what I would do."

Dolores squirm-shifts in her chair. "Now, now, my friend. Perhaps the other woman was just lonely, or maybe Carlitos misled her—sometimes men do. You know how sometimes married men complain that their wives don't behave or don't complete their duties. Maybe this woman believed him and she's lonely."

"Ha. Pretends to believe, I say. And if we can't trust our sisters, what will become of us? Look at you, you're a single woman, but you don't listen to such nonsense—oh, some gossips might say you go out with too many men, but only single men, yes?" When Dolores doesn't respond, she repeats, "Yes?"

Dolores nods. Outside a songbird perches on the rim of the crumbling birdbath, dips its tiny beak into the water, but never takes its glittering eye from Dolores. She rips the last strip of paper from the milk can. "Maybe I *will* visit this Doña Refugio, see what she has to say about my little excursion to Guaymas. Remember, I told you, I made reservations to stay at a little hotel, right there on the beach, during school break. But then I thought maybe I'll cancel. I went there last year for Christmas and it wasn't so good."

"First visit this adviser," Mercy says, "see what she has to say. Who knows? Maybe this time you'll meet a special man. Not one of those tourists looking for sex, like it doesn't exist in their own house—no, no, a nice Mexican man. Someone who needs papers, maybe? Anyway, you need a rest from your students. You have not been yourself for some time now."

"Does this Doña Refugio offer you a commission for bringing her new customers?" Dolores's voice sounds more serious than she intended.

"Ay, Dolores, you always think everything is for money. No, no, it's just that she can help you discover your destiny. Anyway, you are my friend. It's not easy to find friends in this life." She rocks her weight out of the kitchen chair and says, "Well, I'd better get to my washing machine, yes?"

For a moment, Dolores doesn't move; she cannot force her eyes to meet Mercy's. In the garden, the songbird lifts its head and its throat quivers when it warbles a nameless tune that floats away on a shimmer-wave of heat. "Here, let me get that for you," Dolores says and picks up the two pillowcases of laundry. Mercy tries to link arms with her, but Dolores pulls away. "I'm sweating too much," she says.

Minutes later, in the bathroom, Dolores fills the tub, plunges her foot into the near-scalding water. Her torso sinks into the heat, water laps up onto her sides, fluid strands meeting at her waistline and lower, lacing into the mound of hair. Even there she's turning gray. How many men have there been over the years? She never wanted to be like Mercy and all the other women like her: afraid-to-be-alone women who cry over men. She worked her way through college and had no time for relationships. Then as an elementary-school teacher, there were few opportunities to meet men. When she had time after grading papers and running committees, she would drop into bars, driving out of town so she wouldn't run into her students' parents, and later, former students.

Then, somewhere along the path, even before Carlos, the men began to call her only after the bars closed or to meet her in lonely alleys where their wives wouldn't see them. There, they parked their own cars and then sat back in hers while she drove them to her bed. To her bed with the sheets scrubbed free of old sex and prepared for new with a sprinkling of Chanel No. 5.

At first she had liked the relationships: no commitment. She had a need, they had a need. No complications. She was in control. But the circle of men has grown smaller, smaller, and she finds that more and more they expect gifts, even money. When did it change? What was it Carlos said to her last time, after accepting the gold-plated cigarette case and matching lighter? "Don't be so desperate, Dolores, it isn't attractive on a woman."

Even now, immersed in wet heat, she shivers at the thought of those words. But Carlos is wrong, she is not desperate. Not really. It's only that the territory has grown stale, the men of Mesquite take her for granted. She is still attractive, and thirty-nine is still young. Yes, maybe in Guaymas things can be the way they used to be.

She floats her arms on the water, slowly pushes down until the golden bracelets lie beneath the gentle waves, and thinks of treasures sinking down, down in some faraway ocean. If only she could find a new boyfriend, or if she could get a raise, she could buy . . . what? Well, something. That's all she needs to cheer her up, get things back the way they were. Her hands press, fingers spread starlike, onto her belly, push the soft flesh, the emptiness within. Tears slide off both sides of her face, over the throb of her temples, and into the still-steaming bathwater.

"How much farther?" Dolores asks.

A group of barefoot children encircle her, hungry eyes following each swing and bump of her purse. With a lace-trimmed handkerchief she dabs at the sweat on her brow. When she shades her eyes with her hand and looks in the direction of their pointed fingers, she sees the rust-brown tin roofs huddled on a decline.

She nods and licks her lips to keep them from sticking together. After the children snatch the paper pesos she dangles from her fingertips, they run away, brown skin blending into sunbaked hills. She lifts her face to catch a breeze, but it carries the stench of misery (Mercy had warned her about the nearby cesspool), so she pinches her nostrils beneath the balled-up handkerchief and presses on.

She stops in front of a shack with the door cracked and peers into the chasmlike blackness. A tip of a cigarette glows red in the darkness. Maybe this is not the answer, maybe she should turn away.

"Come in, come in," a voice calls from the interior of the shanty. Feet shuffle from the inside and the door opens wide. Doña Refugio peers up at her with eyes squinted to the sun and to the smoke from the cigarette drooping at the right side of her mouth. Her age is uncertain; too much life exposure has leathered the skin, and lines, like deep cuts, fan out from her eyes, which are of an unusual hazel.

Inside the one-room house, Dolores perches on the edge of the wobbly chair that the adviser offers to her and listens to her own uneven breathing. Doña Refugio breaks an egg into a glass of water, studies it, cigarette bobbing between her lips. A long ash drops onto the table; she flicks it onto the plywood floor with a stained fingernail, looks up and stares into Dolores's eyes. "Hmmm," she says and nods slowly, as if what she sees there reaffirms what the egg has told her.

"What's this?" she asks so suddenly that Dolores starts.

Dolores stares hard at the spot that the adviser points out, a red speck in the yolk. "Blood?"

"Of course, blood, that anyone can see." Doña Refugio flicks off another ash. "But more, a bubble of air around it, an emptiness, see? Hmmm, the soul bleeding?"

"A soul bleeding? I don't see any such thing." Dolores's tone makes it clear she doesn't like the direction this conversation is taking. She isn't in the mood for abstractions or philosophical lectures. "I want to know what the future holds," she says. "Something, someone specific."

The adviser makes smacking noises with her lips as she lights another cigarette with the butt of the one that was in her mouth. She sucks the smoke deep into her lungs before exhaling slowing through her nostrils. While she picks specks of tobacco from her lower lip, her eyes move over Dolores's face, study it as though it were a map. The hazel irises of her eyes sparkle, a sparkle that picks up Dolores's reflection, shines it back to her in a glitter of yellow lights. Her gaze drops back to the egg.

"Sí, sí," Doña Refugio mumbles to herself, then louder: "You will find your heart's desire there."

"My true love? Where? In Guaymas?" Dolores leans forward.

The adviser scoots the glass an inch closer to Dolores. "See those little ripples in the white? The ocean. Something more, hmmmm, yes, there it is, an arco iris, a rainbow." She tilts the saucer toward Dolores. "Can you see yourself there?"

"Yes, yes," she says, "it's the name of the hotel, Hotel Arco Iris." Dolores stares harder but still sees only an egg with a speck of blood in it, but she wants the empty coldness to go away. "Go on," she says, "go on."

Doña Refugio slides the egg a bit in the opposite direction. "I see a uniform, an officer, an official, or maybe a waiter. But wait, chula." She holds up her hand, the work-hardened palm creased with dark lines. "Don't put on such a face." She cackles and her hand begins to stroke her own thigh. "Hmmm, very young this new love," she says. Dolores watches the back-and-forth motion of her hand. "A man to cure that longing that wakes you up during the long nights. So long the nights, yes, querida?"

"A man who will be there all night, every night," Dolores says.

"A man of gold, one who will give you what you're looking for," the curandera says, and shuffles in broken-down men's shoes to a crate next to an army cot. She groans when she bends down to lift the crocheted doily that hangs over the side of the crate and pulls out a cigar box. She plucks out a crimson cloth and holds it up by one frayed corner. Dolores stares at it as Doña Refugio walks toward her.

"Here is the real magic," she says, gently waving the red square. "Of course, it will cost extra. I am a poor woman, after all. And you are a person who never underestimates the value of money. Everything has its price—that's what you say, yes?"

"Is it silk?" Dolores says and slides it between her thumb and index finger.

"Almost, almost." Doña Refugio tugs it away from Dolores's grasp.

Dolores pulls bills from her wallet and lays them on the table one by one until the adviser finally nods in agreement.

She pats the sweat from Dolores's face with the scarf, tucks it into the breast pocket of the other woman's blouse, plucks at it so a corner droops out. "Earlier, I treated it with a strong potion of love. Wear it over your heart. It will reveal to all the truth that lies inside."

Two weeks later, after unpacking in Room 19 of the Hotel Arco Iris, Dolores, her high heels a hollow echo on the ceramic tiles, follows the headwaiter through the hotel's dining room. He wears a uniform of bolero jacket and black slacks, but she can tell by the studied sway of his round hips that this one is not for her. He hesitates at a booth, but she shakes her head. "No, there," she says and points to the center of the cavernlike room.

Once her eyes become accustomed to the shadows, she sees many of the regulars she met during last year's Christmas break, now sprinkled around the dark room, each alone at a candlelit table. She shared cocktails with most of them last year, these pilgrims to the Hotel Arco Iris, but something about them, she can't say what, frightens her.

She nods to Bill, a Korean War vet, his wheelchair angle-parked by the wall to keep the passage clear. Last year he had his sleepy attendant push him to Dolores's room at four in the morning, where he cried whiskey tears. He pulled out a tattered lonely-hearts magazine and turned it to the ad he had placed:

FINANCIALLY SECURE American seeks traditional, young Mexican girl for marriage. Must send photograph with first letter. Will pay passage for first meeting with the right gal.

After speaking with him, Dolores discovered that his teenage pen pal had arrived for a meeting expecting to see a tall, young soldier, the man that Bill was before losing the bottom half of his legs in Korea so many years ago. Dolores wonders if this year Bill will meet a girl poor enough to pretend to see him as he wants to be seen.

Her fingertips graze the scarf that she tied into a bow around the spaghetti straps of her sundress, and she lets her gaze roam again. Now it rests on the too-thin businesswoman from Tucson, on her intelligent face that collapses in disillusioned folds. Last visit, her room, two doors down from Dolores's, faced the seashore, and in the evening, the woman, naked from her bath, lay on her bed in the glow of a scarf-covered lamp. And every evening, Dolores peeked through the slats of her own shutters and saw a beach boy's lithe silhouette break away from the moon shadows, slide over the windowsill, and slip into the other woman's room. The young man always left in the still-magical moments before the dawn, no doubt with a little something for his time stuffed inside his swimming trunks.

And over there in the farthest corner sits the history professor from Mexico City, his soft body heaped onto a chair like a melting mound of ice cream. That one never volunteers to join the other pilgrims for a nightcap, tries to avoid them. But Dolores has heard the maids talking and knows that the professor is married and from a respectable family, but comes here to negotiate deals that will soothe the needs that throb through his gnarled veins. Already there is a bruise beneath one eye. It is said that those injuries cost him many extra pesos. How does he explain those souvenirs to his family year after year? Now she can almost feel him shiver with anticipated pain when a muscular young waiter arrives to take his order.

She stares blankly at the end of the room, French doors opened to the terraza. Her thoughts travel outside to the

Chasing Shadows

night, to steps leading to the beach, the lap of ocean waves beyond. Her body fills with a great sadness.

"Would you like another drink, Señora?" A waiter bends over her, so close that his lips tickle the outer rim of her ear.

She jerks away, and he touches her forearm as if to calm her. The hairs on her arm spring up like sentinels. She takes this as a sign: He is the one. Dolores twists her body around so that he can see the scarlet cloth tied in a bow over her heart. He is very young. "Señorita," she corrects him, then adds, "You aren't the same waiter, the one who brought my drinks. I would have remembered you."

"I was already leaving for the day, but I just happened to see you and, pues, something, who can say what, pulled me straight to you, señorita." His words are singsong, like those of a child who has memorized a poem that means more to someone else than to him.

She looks sharply at him, but his face remains smooth and impassive. His finger plays with the edge of her bow, then he cups it in his hand, and a bit of red, like a drop of blood, peeps out between his fingers.

"So pretty," he says, and his lips stretch back over his teeth, more to one side than the other; a smile practiced in the mirror.

When she compliments him on his gold tooth, she hears her own voice and thinks that it trembles as much as her heart.

"Please permit me to join you," he says and pulls out a chair, waits for her answer.

Dolores looks away. The others in the room are watching, the flame from the candle on each table throwing a shadow on each face.

"I would like to order a bottle of Chivas," he says, "but I'm a little low on cash at the moment." He hesitates, adds,

"Maybe some other time." Still standing, he scoots the chair back slightly.

Dolores presses her hand over her eyes and indicates the candle with her chin. "My eyes," she says. "They're delicate, you understand."

He smiles, leans forward, and spits on the tiny flame. It dies with a barely perceptible hiss.

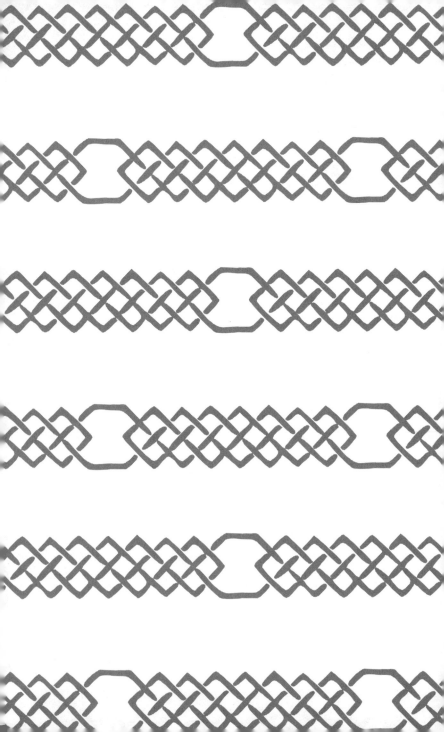

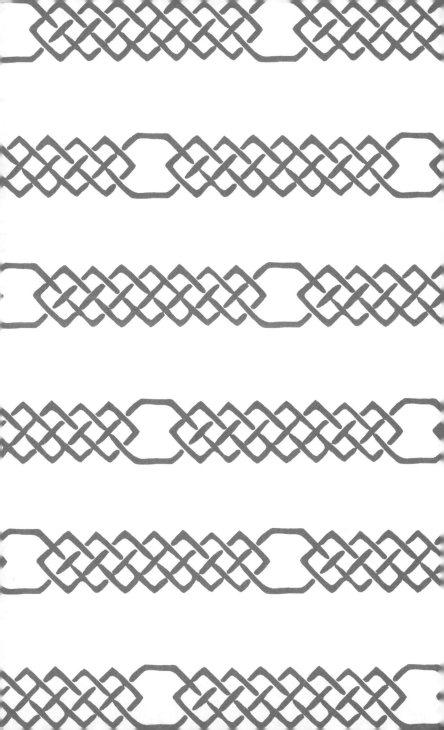

love and happiness

CAREFUL TO NOT KNOCK THE bulging burlap bag slung over his shoulder, Mono pushes through the fingerprint-smudged glass doors of the Mesquite Bus Depot, shuffles his bulk across the waiting room to the edge of the snack shop. The standing fan at one end of the lunch counter whirs the familiar odors across the room: onions, cilantro, and fresh jalapeños, chorizo sizzling in its own fat. He pictures a plate heaped high, eggs scrambled with the spicy sausage, pico de gallo hot sauce on the side. But today is Sunday, the day he visits his sister. She insists he save his hunger for the meal she prepares especially for him, even though he is certain he has room for more in the empty ache that is his stomach.

The scent of chilaquiles hits his senses, and his nostrils flare. He swallows the juices that threaten to overflow the borders of his mouth, gulps of saliva and denied desire. He rolls the heavy bag off his back, sets it gently on the scarred-wood floor. Inside the bag, among the other found goods, lies the special treasure he discovered this week in his rounds as a garbageman. A gift, but for whom? Normally, there would be no question—he would give it to his sister, Fidelina, or her daughter, Eugenia. Things are different now. He sucks in his lips to stop their nervous quivering. Josie will know what to do. She's younger than he is and writes poetry he doesn't understand, but when he listens to her recite, he feels light, weightless, floating on a sea of words.

"It's Sunday, did you forget?" Josie calls from behind the counter. "Today is for visiting la Fidelina, no?" She gestures for Mono to come over.

He pulls off his grease-stained fedora, and with the heel of his palm, rubs the slight indentation that the too-tight hat has left across his forehead. His friends tease him for wearing such a silly thing, especially since he wasn't able to find one large enough for his head. Sombrero de maricón, they say, hat of a fairy. But he avoids mirrors and imagines himself looking like Humphrey Bogart. Josie tells him the fedora looks distinguished, a good thing for a man his age. So when his compadres tease, he merely stares down at his feet and smiles, a small lonely tug, a Bogart expression.

Hat in one hand and bag in the other, he walks to the counter. There he balances his weight on a stool, separates his legs to accommodate his stomach, waits for Josie to bring him coffee and advice. Today he'll tell her about his Esperanza. So far, he has told no one, afraid he was only imagining things again. Could it really be that after forty years of loneliness, he has met a woman who smiles at him with her eyes? Until now Fidelina was the only woman who ever loved him. Not even his mother loved him. He couldn't really remember her, since she died before he was two, but Fidelina always explains to him how things are. That's why he hasn't told her about the woman he has met. What if his sister—so much smarter than he—insists on convincing him that Esperanza's kind words are nothing more than charity, or worse, a joke to share with friends behind his back? Fidelina's capacity for detecting hypocrisy in others always amazes him, but, in truth, there have been times when he can't see the bad in others, even when she points it out to him. Mono sucks hard on his lower lip.

"What do you have in there today?" Josie says as she sets the mug of coffee in front of him. "So tight you're holding on to it, like maybe you got love and happiness in there." She smiles and looks down at his hand, still clutching the neck of the bag.

He rolls his shoulders, embarrassed to speak, certain his voice will squeak the way it always does when he is nervous. He glances around, makes certain no one is watching (better Fidelina doesn't know about his find in case he decides it's not for her). With both hands, he reaches down into the bag, gently lifts a package, a folded paper sack from the Safeway market. After sliding it onto the counter, he pulls at the string tied around it. His hands tremble and he cannot untie the double bow. He lifts his forearm, swipes at the sweat sliding from his scalp into his eyebrows, waits as Josie takes over. Once the string lies in a small heap, he unfolds the brown paper, brings out something wrapped in layers of crepe paper, passion-red.

He drinks the coffee, burns his lips, his throat, but he doesn't take his eyes off Josie's face. When her eyebrows lift and her lips circle, "Ooh," he covers his mouth to muffle the giggle that escapes.

The silver of the vanity set gleams up at them with all the easy self-confidence of beauty. His wavy reflection— carnival-glass distorted—returns his gaze from the polished metal. He quickly looks away, pulls back his head until his face no longer mocks him. After all, his nickname isn't El Mono, the Ape, for nothing. His gaze darts about, lands on the pie case, pecan is the special today, one of his favorites, gooey, sticks to his insides, stays with him longer. Should he risk ordering a slice? No, someone might see him, tell Fidelina he didn't save his appetite for her.

"Ay, hombre," Josie says and pulls his thoughts away from the pie. She runs her finger along the fancy design etched in the back of the mirror. "Don't tell me this is from your job?"

"Yes, yes," he says and laughs, for he, too, can't believe his good fortune. He explains how the pieces were buried in the Lapuentes' garbage, strewn among the newspapers, orange rinds, and coffee grounds. He tells her how the back of the mirror, brush, and comb were somewhat tarnished, but he rubbed them in cream polish and buffed them with a soft cloth. "You see, like they've never been used, but anyway, I cleaned the bristles—and the comb, too—with Clorox. And the mirror glass was broken in many pieces. But I glued in another one, a little smaller than the original, but it looks okay, no?" He holds it up for her inspection, angles it away from his face. "You see? Almost like new."

"For your sister, of course. Or maybe your niece?" Josie says, for like all Mesquite, she knows Mono gives the best to his family. It has always been that way, even before Fidelina's husband, Samuel, deserted her and Eugenia last year. Although once it became clear that Samuel was not returning, Fidelina became even more dependent on Mono's paycheck, and his weekly gifts are no longer mere luxuries. But now things are different.

Mono shrugs. "Pues, that's what I don't know for sure. Maybe I'm going to give it to someone else." He laughs, a quavering sound, unsure, and studies Josie's face for reaction. Better to know now if the idea is ridiculous, if he would only be playing the fool once more.

Josie lowers her chin and peers at him from beneath the blackness of her eyebrows. "Not for Fidelina this time?"

He holds her gaze until his lips tremble. Josie comes around the counter and sits on the stool next to him. "Ay, ay, ay, hombre, tell me all about it."

He blinks twice, whispers, in a distant voice, thin and high, "Esperanza, that's her name."

Josie pours cream into his cup. "Esperanza," she repeats, "Hope, a good name."

He sips the coffee, closes his eyes, pictures it all in his mind again before he tells her the story: It was during his collection route in a middle-class suburb, nowhere near Fidelina's apartment on Frontera Street. Chucho, the garbage truck driver, turned onto the cul-de-sac, slowing down as they approached the Ortegas'. But it wasn't Mrs. Ortega coming out of the house this time.

A stranger, short and sturdy, pushed, pulled, and half-carried the large metal trash can to the end of the yard. She glanced up and smiled at Mono when he hung out from his place at the back of the truck, called for her to wait for his help. The sun reflected off the aluminum can, blinded him, and for a second, he would later say, he thought he had been struck by lightning. But instead, it was his Esperanzita, shining such a bright light onto his life, that a vision appeared before his eyes, a path leading into the future. The light shone even brighter when he later found out that the Ortegas had hired her to clean their house on a permanent basis. His little Hope was in Mesquite to stay.

"I heard that part," he explains to Josie, "about love striking like lightning in some movie—I can't remember which one—but that about the light and the trash can, pues, that's my own thinking. But it really happened, don't think I am pretending."

Josie nods. "You don't have to tell me that, I see truth in your eyes." She rewraps the set slowly, says, "A nice gift if a man wants to declare his love to a woman, yes?"

"Yes, yes," he says, "my thoughts also."

"And Fidelina," Josie says, patting the package, "does she know about this?"

The mention of his sister's name reminds him of the time, and Mono presses the hat back on his head, shifts his weight. He understands the problem as clearly as Josie. If Fidelina knows he has found something so valuable, she will not understand how he could give it to anyone else. She'll cry, ask him if he enjoys making her suffer, tossing her aside for some cualquiera who will never love him the way his sister does. For after all, she has always been there for him. It's true that sometimes others find his sister a difficult person; some have hinted that perhaps she does not have his best interests in mind. He refuses to listen to this talk. Hasn't Fidelina always looked out for him?

Outside, the Greyhound bus *hiss*-brakes to the curb. Josie squeezes his hand and returns behind the counter, fills water glasses, places them on a tray in preparation for the travelers. She asks him to wait—they can talk after her new customers are taken care of, but Mono glances at the wall clock, shakes his head. Fidelina is waiting.

Eyes fixed on the scene outside the open window of his Ford, Mono sucks on his lower lip. His gaze travels through a grove of mesquite trees, across the dust of Frontera Street, to the redbrick apartment. Upstairs, Fidelina probably stands over her stove, in spite of the Arizona heat, taking a taste of something delicious bubbling in a pot, some delicacy prepared for him, her only brother.

The fingers of Mono's hand encircle, slide back and forth on the sweat-slick steering wheel. His gaze jumps to the burlap bag, an itchy pile on the front seat next to him. Fidelina or Esperanza? A rumble deep inside his intestines reminds him of his hunger and Fidelina's cooking. He kneads his stomach to ease the emptiness.

For a moment, his eyes close, and he imagines Esperanza sitting at a dresser—one of those frill-covered tables like in the movies—brushing her dark brown hair, holding up the hand mirror so she can see the back of her head. He hesitates only a second before pulling out the Safeway bag and sliding it under the front seat. Pushing his fedora farther down onto his head, he grabs the burlap bag and steps out of his car.

As he strides across Frontera Street, he glances up at the sky as if he expects it to reflect the sense of wonderment and magic that he feels when he thinks of Esperanza. But the heavens haven't changed—the sky is a typically too-beautiful-to-be-true Arizona blue. The glare brings tears to his eyes. He shoots a parting glance over the slope of his shoulder at the Ford. Suddenly he wants to jump back in and speed away to Esperanza now, instead of waiting for tonight, when she has agreed to go with him to the cinema. He stops in the middle of the road, almost loses himself to his favorite daydream: he and Esperanza, sitting side by side in the darkened show, he reaching for her hand, interlacing his fingers with hers. He wonders if he should rub deodorant on his palms to keep them from sweating. But this is not the time for such thoughts. His mind turns to the bag on his back; he rolls the burden of its weight to the other side.

Moments later, he peers through the kitchen screen door and calls out, "It's your hermanito. I bring you wonderful surprises."

"Pssst," Fidelina hisses from the darker interior of the apartment, "do you have to make announcements for the whole world to hear?" Her leather sandals *snip-snap* against her calloused heels as she crosses the room. She holds the door open and slips the bag from his grip. When he kisses the side of her upraised face, he feels her stiffness, sees that she looks away instead of smiling up at him.

"You are late," she says. "Don't think I didn't see you out there in your car, wasting your time with daydreams, like always. Well, what are you waiting, little brother? Sit down, your food is ready."

At the kitchen table, Fidelina places a steaming bowl of pozole stew, thick with pork and hominy, before him. "There's everything you need," she says, and with her chin, points to the saucers of shredded lettuce, sliced radishes, and lime wedges sitting in the center of the table. "The hot sauce I made fresh today, especially for you."

He has just sprinkled lettuce and radishes on his stew when Fidelina says, "Wipe your face." She sits down across from him, hands him a paper napkin. "You're sweating even more than usual. Something has upset you?"

"It's too hot today," he says.

"No hotter than usual."

He stirs the pozole, feels her probing gaze on him, but doesn't look up. If she sees his eyes, his lips that won't be still, she'll know he's hiding something from her. Just as he spoons the first bite into his mouth, she says, "You know I have always wanted what's best for you, yes?"

He nods slowly and chews on a bite of tortilla.

Fidelina squeezes a wedge of lime into his bowl. "You didn't put any. What are you thinking today?" She traces her fingertip around the edge of the saucer, and he watches. Round and round her finger goes. When he says nothing, she continues, "You know, I am not an educated woman, but I hope that you have enough respect for me that you can see I have some intelligence."

Something is wrong, he knows it. Maybe one of the gossips has told her something, but what? Better to wait and see. He stirs a heaping tablespoon of hot sauce into his pozole, slurps the broth. "Ay." He fans at his mouth with his hand. "Dios mío, what kind of chile did you put in that sauce? It's taking the skin off my tongue."

Fidelina slides her Pepsi across the table to him. As he guzzles the soda, Fidelina says, "You see, anything I have is yours, hermanito." He sets the bottle down, moves to push it back. "No, no," she says, "keep it, I begrudge you nothing."

"Gracias, gracias," Mono mumbles, thinks of the vanity set beneath the seat of his car. Who else knew about it? Roberto Sepeda. Yes, he saw when Mono dug it out of the trash, before he had a chance to stuff it all beneath his shirt. Maybe he mentioned it to his wife, Mirna. There was always a competition for who could find the best throwaways.

"You know, it's strange," Fidelina continues. "I've been so sentimental today, thinking about our childhood. Do you ever think about those days?"

"Hmmm, not too much," Mono says.

"Remember how you got your nickname?" Her fingertip returns to the saucer's ridge.

"Sure, sure, everybody knows." He has heard that story too many times. He glances around the room in search of another topic. "Why not see what I brought you?" he says.

"I was already five when you were born, so naturally I remember it all very well," Fidelina says. "Poor Mami, her heart was so weak—died before you were two. Can you imagine what our father said about you?"

He nods, tries to smile, but his lips quiver too much, refuse to obey.

"Pues, he claimed that you were born so ugly, it put a strain on Mami's heart and killed her." Fidelina laughs delicately. "Ay, that Papi. Anyway, he nicknamed you El Mono.

Naturally it never mattered to me that others laughed at you—that is to say, it didn't change my feelings for you. Well, we're the same blood, after all, and we have to look out for each other."

"The same blood," he repeats.

Fidelina rearranges the condiments, lines them in a row, then puts them back into a circle, while he watches. "Yes, I have always been there for you, and now that I am alone, you help me. Such a good brother," she says. She reaches for the bag and drags it across the linoleum toward her, sets it next to her chair. "To be honest," she says, "I know what you are so nervous about. It was going to be a surprise, no?"

He doesn't answer, gobbles the pozole. Starving, he's starving. She continues. "Mirna Sepeda, she tells me that maybe you won't give it to me, says maybe you even want to hide it from me, your own sister. And this even you won't believe. . . ." She leaves the sentence hanging between them while she gets up to serve him more stew.

His spoon reaches for the bowl even before she sets it back down. "She—Mirna, I mean—she says to me, Maybe he's going to give that set to somebody else, maybe your brother has himself a little girlfriend. But I say, How can that be? Eh? Pues, I say to Mirna, you know how women are these days, leading a poor man on, using him for his paycheck. They fill his head with pretty lies. Yes, hermanito, I said lies, sweet words and gestures to confuse you."

Mono remembers Esperanza looking up at him, sideways, from the corners of her eyes. At the time, she seemed shy, kind, even a little lonely. And she was nervous when he talked to her, stammered until he forgot his own nervousness. But maybe Fidelina is right, it's just an act.

"Such women," Fidelina says, "only want to take everything the man has, then what? Poof, gone. But a sister's love? Well, that don't never change."

Mono tries to look away, but Fidelina reaches out, clutches his jaw, holds his face and his gaze. He wants to answer that he will always love her, but that now he will share his love, but the words lose their way in the grumble of his insides.

"Or maybe now I'm old, you will leave me, too?" Fidelina's chin quivers. "Well?"

Mono shakes his head.

"You're a good man," she says, releases his face. She holds the mouth of the bag open with both hands, pulling one side and then the other to better see inside. "Pues, where is it?"

"In the car," he says after a pause.

Fidelina looks back up at him. "Well?" she says when he doesn't move. He holds on to the edge of the table and pushes himself up with a sigh.

Moments later, when he bends over and reaches across and under the car seat for the package, his heavy heart feels as if it will drop out of his chest onto the floor. He lifts out the mirror, and a tear, hot with his pain and slick with the oil gathered from his cheek, rolls down into the corner of his mouth. He flicks the drop of liquid into his mouth with the tip of his tongue and waits as the saltiness dissolves into his saliva—just as he has done so many times before.

He unwraps the mirror, strokes the silver. When he glances at it, it is not his reflection he sees, but Esperanza's, and on her face, that same sweet smile she always greets him with. He looks away quickly, afraid to watch her face fade. He slides the key into the ignition. Maybe Josie can help him find the words to explain to Fidelina.

Cloud-Shadow

FLACO LIES FACE TO FOOT IN the army cot he shares
with his older-by-eleven-months brother, stares into the
predawn gray, awaits the sun to illuminate the room. At last
the glow of day comes and, *easy, easy,* he inches his elbow
from beneath Riquis's calf, hopes his brother is not just
feigning sleep. Flaco has permission to leave—well, he'll
turn twelve next month, almost a man—but his mother
warned him to not wake up Olga, asleep in the crib only
four feet from the cot, or the new baby in the adjacent
room with his parents.

One last gentle tug, and he's free, out from beneath the
covers, pulls on his jeans, T-shirt, kneels beside the bed to
tie his shoes, just like today was the same as any other day.
As if nothing had changed, as if his heart hadn't been
ripped from his chest, fed to the Sun God; his heart into the
mouth-gaping center; his heart, *smash, smash,* pulverized,
fire-red shreds clinging, dropping; his heart, blood-rain
dripping onto the desert sand. He leans his head against
the mattress, cannot will back the single tear that trickles
from the outer corner of one eye.

It is then Riquis slaps the side of Flaco's head, *hiss*-
whispers, "Qué pasa, crybaby, what's up?"

Flaco avoids his brother's gaze, shrugs, desperate, certain Riquis will get louder, start Olga screaming, anything to give him a hard time. Then what? His mother will jump out of bed, won't let him leave, and he'll be here when Tonantzin drops by from her apartment just around the corner, knocking at his door like she's making him some big favor or something. Ha, that's what she thinks, but he doesn't care about her. That's right, nada, nothing, not even one little bean does he care.

When Riquis remains silent, Flaco glances at him, but his brother only watches, studies his face. He expects that at any moment Riquis will lift one corner of the blanket, fart all that gas that he carries around—like he's a time bomb waiting to go off—which will surely startle Olga. Instead, Riquis says, "See, brother, I told you not to be such a pendejo. Ain't no such thing as love. Why can't you never just accept your fate, eh?"

Riquis's voice comes out soft, tired, gives Flaco the courage to answer. "I make my own fate," he says.

"Yeah, you and Jesus Christ, and look what happened to him," Riquis says, fake-laughs out one side of his mouth. Olga shifts, grunts, and they both shut up, watch her until she sighs, curls back into her dreams. Then Riquis flops on his side to face the wall, waves his hand behind him, dismisses Flaco.

Far beyond the Frontera Street apartment, Flaco scrambles up the steep incline of his favorite hill, grabs on to the craggy face, fingers and sneakered-toes, pulls himself to the top, stands, looks out over the desert. With his forearm, he swipes the sweat from his face and gazes down on the valley he has climbed out of: Mesquite, land of his raza, now in Arizona, once Mexico, and before, when it simply was. He will never leave. He opens his arms wide as if to embrace the whole town, his brother, all the townspeople, except for her: Tonantzin.

A gust of wind wobbles his balance, and he lowers himself to a crouch. When he does, the rolled-up sheaf of papers in the back pocket of his jeans almost pushes out. He reaches around, clutches one end tightly so the folded sheets of notebook paper will not blow away, smooths out the handmade comic book, flips through the pages. Hadn't he written this issue especially for her? El Poder—caped hero with the combined looks and abilities of El Santo, El Zorro, and Superman—saves a beautiful woman from a horrible fate.

On the woman's right cheek, near the curve below her eye, he had drawn a heart-shaped beauty mark, like Tonantzin's, and, around her neck, a tiny hummingbird on a silver chain, like the one she always wears. In the end El Poder and the woman fall in love, and it is understood that they will stay together, forever.

What a pendejo he'd been, just like Riquis said. He rolls the comic, slaps it into his palm, brings it to his eye, gazes through it, back toward Frontera Street. If he were truly El Poder, he would be able to see the apartment, X-ray-vision the walls, her bedroom, her face, her eyes, closed. Soon she will be no more, gone, her mirada, her gaze, as shut off to him as if she were dead and buried, like their neighbor Lázaro Sandoval, who, last week, at twenty-six finally died from the injuries of an accident he'd had two years ago.

Since it was known that most of Frontera Street would attend the viewing and later the velorio for Lázaro, Flaco had planned to give the comic to her then; he knew he would have a chance to be alone with her that night. She would read the story he had written and understand that it was his declaration of love.

But he hadn't given her the comic, will never give it to her. Their time together was over, clock broken, gone, finished, forever.

The night of the viewing, Flaco's mother had laid out the clothes: his best jeans and a dress shirt passed down from Riquis, cuffs frayed but bleached so white you hardly noticed. Normally, he didn't like dressing *decent,* as his mother called it, but that night he wanted to be certain that Tonantzin understood he was not playing around, that he, his declaration, were to be taken seriously. Sure, they were young, that he understood, but time meant nothing, time they had to spare.

He ran his finger along the crease his mother had ironed into his jeans, pulled them on over his legs, bath-damp, then, in his parents' dresser mirror, studied the dark hairs above his upper lip as he buttoned the shirt—all the way to the neck-choking top, and without complaint. Then he stepped back, measured out into his palm his father's Brylcreem, just a dab like the advertisement said, was rubbing it into his hair when Riquis jumped through the doorway.

"Why you getting all dressed up like a maricón to impress a dead man?" Riquis said. "He can't see nothing."

Flaco squinted in the mirror, avoided his brother's always-cynical expression, determined that that night not even Riquis could goad him into a fight. "I'm just trying to have a little respect for the dead," Flaco said, which was, after all, also partly true. He slid the comb through his hair, tried to get it to lie in the style of his teenage friend Joaquín. "You know," he continued absentmindedly, "Lázaro was so young, but just like that he's dead. You should think about it."

Riquis shoved him from the mirror's view. "What the fuck is that supposed to mean? Everybody dies, stupid, or maybe you think you're special, like them old-lady gossips." His voice strained falsetto, he said, "Ay, comadrita, that Lázaro, he's too-young-to-die-but-at-least-he-can't-suffer-no-more, and anyway-now-he's-paying-for-all-them-sins." Voice changing back, only angrier: "Like maybe they don't commit no sins, like they ain't gonna die, like they can do something to change time. You know something, little brother? You're the one that better think about it, better quit all the time re-peating shit that everybody says."

Riquis's voice broke and Flaco glanced at him, just long enough to see his brother's red-shot eyes. But he knew bet-ter than to mention it, to even suggest that maybe his brother wasn't so hard like he wanted to be. It was Riquis who used to watch when Lázaro's wife, Amparo, would push him outside in his wheelchair, park him in the dirt yard behind the apartments. Sometimes Riquis would join him, sit on a wooden crate turned on its side, and the two would remain there, quiet, eyes unfathomable gazing to-ward the distant hills, dusk-shadows lengthening, reaching, finally enveloping them.

Flaco moved back to the mirror, focused on only his own reflection, gave Riquis time to wipe his eyes. He ran the spine of the comb down the top center of his head, pulled a few hairs down onto his forehead. Riquis's hand darted out, ruffled Flaco's hair. "What? You think you look like your big hero Joaquín? He's another one that's going to find out what's what someday, him with all his causes. Look out for número uno—that's my motto—and live for today, because tomorrow . . . well."

Riquis began to dance around, bounced on the balls of his feet, slap-punched Flaco's face, but not as hard or with as much energy as usual, more like just paying tribute to a habit. "Your little girlfriend's going to be there, right?" *Slap.* "Someday you guys gonna get married and live happy ever after, just like in the fairy tales, that right, fairy?" *Slap, slap.*

Then just as suddenly as he had started shadowboxing, Riquis stopped, turned away. "He's dead—big deal. Anyway, nobody wanted him around—like they might catch his pain, or something—maybe they're glad he's dead," he said. "Me, I'm getting out of this hole—Mesquite ain't big enough for me—soon as I'm sixteen and can break out of school, three more years, brother, and I'm gone—the marines, French Foreign Legion, who cares?"

Riquis had talked about leaving Mesquite before; so did a lot of the townspeople, and some actually did, in search of jobs, adventures, who knew what else. But when Flaco looked at his brother's face that day, he realized, for the first time, that it was true: Someday Riquis would be gone, they would be separated by space, time.

In the Orozco Funeral Home, at the back of the room, Flaco sat in a wooden folding chair, Tonantzin in the seat next to him, side by side, legs inches above the floor. He patted his chest, his heart, made certain the comic still lay between his jacket and shirt, above the *tick-tick* of his life-pulse. The drawings were the best he'd ever done. Someday he'd be a famous artist, even one of his teachers had said so, and he'd buy a ranch—he'd already picked out the exact land—with a big house on it for the wife and children he would have. He watched Tonantzin's leg swing back and forth—a pendulum—synchronized the movement of his own leg with hers, imagined them as one, and with that illusion his thoughts floated away on a river, heart-red, sea-deep with love eternal.

With his eyes, he willed Tonantzin to look at him, but her gaze moved over Lázaro, upper body slightly elevated, satin-nested, hands crossed, crystal rosary glinting, winking. "So young to die," Flaco says.

"When it's time to leave ... pues." Her voice drifted away with a shrug of her shoulders, sad, accepting. Then, not even changing the tone of her voice, she said, "I'm leaving Mesquite next Saturday."

She said it so sweet-soft that Flaco only stared at her, waited for her to say more, certain he must have misunderstood. "It's time to go to Superior and be with my mother now," she said, and for a moment Flaco forgot how to breathe.

She continued on, while he watched her lips, saw each word slip out like a vapor, clouds of poison dissolving, disappearing into the air; told him how her father had a girlfriend and this Marisol would be doing his cleaning and cooking so he wouldn't need Tonantzin's help anymore, and she should return to her mother, help care for her little brothers and sisters, said it calm with no tears in her voice, like it was nothing, nothing.

She sighed, turned back, faced the front, clasped her hands beneath her chin as if she were praying, and, in that moment, a piece of Flaco's soul died, shriveled, drifted away, lost itself in the cloud-scent of a dead man's flowers.

Now Flaco glances down the steep slope of the hill, determined to stay here for all the hours it takes until Tonantzin has left the apartments for her new life, new friends in Superior. He flips through the comic book, glad he kept it the night of the viewing. Why should she know what he feels? Why reveal his soul to such a girl? Maybe she don't even want to remember him, maybe she wants to forget him like a pain, or even worse, maybe she won't even have to forget him because he ain't really never been in her heart. He rolls the comic, smacks it into his palm, harder,

harder, unrolls. He tears the comic in half, plans to continue, shred it, throw it into the wind, watch it blow away. But he can't.

He stuffs the halves back into his pocket, sits quietly like he was just another grain of Arizona sand; or a tree, mesquite, paloverde, cypress; or a cactus, saguaro, barrel, nopal. He lifts his eyes to the mountain across the valley; a shadow drapes over the summit, starts down. For some reason, he is reminded of the Western movies he has seen with Riquis at the Roxy in downtown Mesquite. Vaqueros, cowboys, Indians, warriors all, once locked in battle against one another—brave shades of black, brown, white—now without color, one spirit-shadow together in time; once-thundering ghost-warriors now silently racing down the mountainside, through the desert, eternal.

He coughs, clears his throat of dust, thinks of yelping the way his father does when he listens to the music of the mariachis. That grito would capture his feelings exactly. But the day's too hot, his throat too dry to shout; he feels parched inside, cracking apart like the earth during the drought season.

He stares at the ground and thinks of all the times his feet have stood on this same spot, all the times he has fought, played with his brother, and other times, with her, Tonantzin. The land hasn't changed; with them, without them, it is still his tierra. He looks away. Something moving in the distance? He lifts both hands, gazes out beneath their shade. At first he thinks it is only another shadow on the earth but no, it is her tiny form, walking steady, true, toward him. What a deception; she isn't true, she's an ingrata, a traidora.

He thinks of running down the other side of the hill, hiding in the grove of pines below, but no. Deep inside, hasn't he known all along that she would come to him, to this hill they have climbed so many times before? And hasn't he been waiting for her, as if he knew this would be his destiny? He blinks the sweat off his eyelashes, keeps his steady gaze on her.

When she starts up the incline, he edges down, meets her halfway.

"Your brother told me to look for you here," she says, then points to the distant sky. "Look at those clouds. Maybe rain's coming, what do you think?"

Flaco glances into the distance but for a moment says nothing, afraid the great balloon of sadness inside him will burst. "Look," he whispers finally, "a sun-shadow. It's going to pass in front of us."

She smiles. "Silly, it's the shadow of a cloud, a cloud-shadow."

The wind increases and the shadow travels faster. He shrugs. "Maybe it's the same thing."

"What do you mean?"

He shakes his head. "I don't know, really, only that without one, you can't have the other." She laughs, hollow. He laughs, hollow echo.

"Want to catch it?" she says, tenses her muscles, prepares to race against him.

He grabs her hand, fingers intertwined. "Together," he says and pushes off on the balls of his feet, hard, as if their future depended on it. Down the hill, faster, faster, until she stumbles, drops to one knee, but he pull-drags her up. "Hurry, hurry," he shouts, "we're almost there, muchacha."

They run, pant, nose into the patch of moving darkness, reach out their free fingers. A blast of wind blows away the cloud and along with it the shadow. They stand, panting, gasping, chests heaving.

"Nothing," Flaco says, "you can't touch it, can't hold it." He releases her hands, stretches his fingers open, shows her the empty palm. "You saw me reach for it, but see, wasn't nothing there. Anyway, it doesn't matter."

She gazes back at him, sad tug-twitch at the corner of her mouth. He looks away, notices her knee, scraped, blood trickling—desert dirt mixing—down her leg. "You see," he says, "how can you leave? Your blood is here, too, this tierra."

"I can't do nothing," she says.

He pulls out the two pieces of the torn comic, hands them to her. "The story will tell you what's in my heart," he says. "Sorry it's torn, an accident." He laughs, hollow. She laughs, hollow echo.

"Toma, take this," she says, and when he looks, she is removing the silver chain from around her neck, holds it out to him.

She presses the chain and tiny hummingbird into the center of his palm, blood-pulse throbbing. He knows its story, how her grandmother gave it to her, told her it was the soul of a dead Aztec warrior, resurrected in the form of that tiny bird.

"I can't," he whispers. "It's yours."

She presses harder still. Is it burning into his flesh, or does he only imagine the pain?

"Take care of it for me," she says. "Now you know, someday I will come back, and if you are still here, well."

"I'll always be here."

She shrugs. "Quién sabe, who knows?"

He listens to her breath, not yet regular. "Quién sabe," he says.

He fists his hand around the hummingbird and shuts his eyes, keeps them closed as if to lock in the memory of this moment. He imagines the hummingbird in flight, inside the colorful armor, green, black, purple. He sees a face, his, his brother's; inside the tiny body, her heart, his heart, heart of Mesquite—clock without hands—beating forever, *tick-tick* eternal.

return of the Spirit

FROM HER FRONT DOOR, Consuelo de la Torre and the new neighbor, Esperanza, gaze at the dead rooster and Esperanza's fiancé, Mono. He stands in the side lot, his arm extended in front of him, fingers clutching the legs of the upside-down, still-twitching headless bird. Mono calls out, "For our wedding tomorrow, Esperanzita." He directs the blood streaming from the neck, marks a cross in the sand, mumbles, "In the name of the Father, the Son, and the Holy Ghost." The rooster, wings outspread, stretches toward the ground, and the ever-thirsty earth absorbs its blood.

Several children gather, watch. Silent. Flaco, Consuelo's favorite neighborhood child, lies on the up-slope behind the apartments, lifts his head to watch below. He's too close to the house at the top of the hill, Consuelo thinks, up there where the woman they call La Malinche lives. It is said that although this Malinche originally emigrated from Mexico, she thinks she is more gringa than the gringas themselves. And more important, she betrays her own people, watches the border fence next to the apartments with her binoculars, reports any attempts of Mexicans to cross into the U.S. Maybe when she looks down here, she's spying on more than the illegals, Consuelo has said. But Consuelo's son, Joaquín, says no, even invited the woman—Cookie

McDonald, she calls herself—and her daughter, Nancy, to tomorrow's wedding reception.

Consuelo stares up at the house for the telltale glint of binocular lenses. Nothing. She cracks open the door, waves her arm until Flaco turns his head toward her. She signals him to come closer, but he holds up his hand, motions *in a while*. Since his little girlfriend Tonantzin moved away from the apartments, he has become more distant.

Before, he used to visit with Consuelo, sit at her kitchen table, and drink coffee, pale and thick with Nestlé's sweetened condensed milk. Now maybe he thinks he is becoming too much of a man for woman talk, instead waits for Joaquín to advise. Many times she has seen them walking together, sometimes serious, sometimes laughing, as if Flaco were a son, learning, the father preparing him for life's responsibilities. La sombra de Joaquín, the shadow of Joaquín, the neighbors have named him.

But Joaquín has not yet returned from his last trip. Two days late already.

Consuelo looks away, returns her attention to Mono. He shakes the rooster one last time, turns slowly, work boots scuffing up dust, holds the bloodless carcass high and makes a victory sign with his free hand.

Esperanza smiles, nudges Consuelo. "So brave," Esperanza says.

"Yes, how sad, such a beautiful animal."

Esperanza laughs. "No, not the rooster. Mono. And look how he concerns himself for my safety," she says. "You heard before how he insisted I stand inside your apartment, *and* behind the screen door."

Consuelo nods. Earlier, Esperanza explained that Doña Pilar, from down the street, had asked Mono to kill her rebellious rooster. It was a magnificent bird, but it would not stay in its own yard, would not stop drawing attention to itself, chasing, pecking passersby. But the old woman also warned Esperanza to keep her distance when Mono did what had to been done, said it's bad luck for a woman of childbearing age to stand too close to the dying.

"But sometimes I don't know about that Doña Pilar," Esperanza says. "She's a little, you know." She points her index finger to her temple, circles.

Consuelo shrugs, says, "Many years ago, before she lost her daughter, she didn't go around talking to the wind. But after Margarita disappeared, Pilar changed. Now they say she's like La Llorona, roaming, searching for her child. How can a mother accept losing her own blood, eh?"

Mono coughs loudly, draws the women's attention back to him. He straightens now, puffs his chest. "Time to return this wild thing—"

"Which you have tamed," Esperanza says, interrupting.

Mono bites his full lips, stops the unmanly giggle. "Now to Doña Pilar and her pots and pans," he says. "Better for us, Esperanzita, a soup to give us strength for tomorrow." He ducks his head, turns away quickly.

Consuelo imagines that beneath his dark skin, he blushes like an innocent. The garbageman often says he still cannot believe that at forty, he finally found a woman to love him. A patient man. Sometimes patience is best, Consuelo thinks. Isn't that what she told Joaquín before he left this time? He had insisted on going against her wishes, argued that she herself had told him since he was a tiny boy that it was his destiny to help his people.

It is true. Of her five children, he is the most like her, and she has always guided him toward fulfilling the dreams she once held for herself, to become the person she might have been had she been born with the freedom of a man.

Study law, she always tells him. First pull yourself out of the pit, then you will be in a better position to help the rest of us. Forget the illegal operations, they are too dangerous.

And, during their last conversation, she reminded him that the migra almost caught him on his last trip across the border. It's as if they knew when to expect him. And his friends who come to visit him, now they tell him they think they are being followed. It's as if their moves are being reported.

Let someone else help this group cross into the land of hope and illusion, she said, and told him of her nightmare: She had seen him lying alone—no admirers surrounding him to listen to his Aztec-proud words, or to catch the warmth of his inner light. Alone. A death-limp body left on the desert floor, his face so pale it seemed as though his tan were only fading paint, translucent in the glow of the ghostly white moon. Fingers of dark shadow appeared out of the north, hovered above the earth, suddenly gathered, ominous clouds, shaping, inching through the twilight, finally enveloping Joaquín. It's just a dream, Mamá, he told her, but she saw how, for just a second, he looked away, gazed at some specter crossing his line of vision.

Consuelo clutches the front of her dress, fingertips press into her breast. If only she could reach her heart, tear it out before someone else does it for her with news she still hopes she will not be given. She turns back into the kitchen, toward the table, wants to concentrate on food, stacks onto a platter sweet-bean tamales, childhood favorites prepared especially for Joaquín. Esperanza walks behind her, steps on her heel.

Consuelo wishes the bride-to-be would go back to her own apartment; the woman talks too much, and Consuelo needs to be alone with her thoughts. Her husband, Rogelio, teases her, says their house has more traffic than the snack shop at the Mesquite Bus Depot, that if Consuelo charged for all the comfort and cups of coffee she has offered over the years, they would be rich.

Esperanza follows her to the table, picks up a bag of pinto beans, pours a pile onto the oilcloth, sorts out pebbles, tiny twigs, says, "I heard his ghost again last night."

For just a second, before she realizes Esperanza is picking up the thread of an earlier conversation, Consuelo's heart stops. It is a story she has already heard: the tale of Lázaro, the former tenant of the apartment Esperanza and Mono will share after tomorrow. Until his death a month ago, Consuelo, too, heard Lázaro. That was before he became a phantom and could still scream out during the long nights for mercy, finally, at the end, begging God to release him from his pain-dominated body.

Esperanza swipes beans into the pot on her lap, clasps her hands in prayer before she imitates the moans of anguish she swears she heard last night in her bedroom. "*Aay, aaay, aaaayyy.* Like a dying man gargling blood." She pulls a small bottle of holy water from her apron pocket, unscrews the top, tips the bottle to her finger, streaks a fast-drying cross in the center of her forehead.

When Esperanza opens her mouth to repeat the howl, Consuelo covers her ears. "Enough, my friend, let the dead rest."

"But he can't," Esperanza says. "That's the problem." She holds out the bottle she clutches in her fist. "Don't be afraid, sprinkle some agua sagrada all around your apartment, don't forget the corners. Me, I been doing it the whole week I'm living there. I tell you death is near. Don't you feel it?"

"No," Consuelo says, too loud, wraps her arms around herself. "You only think this because you know that he died in your apartment. That is all it is, nothing more."

"Hmmm, perhaps," Esperanza says, "but you must admit, if we consider the life that Lázaro lived, then his death was justo; he found what he was looking for."

"Let's have some compassion for the dead," Consuelo says.

"What compassion? I only say the truth. A man's death must suit his life. And that man did a lot of maldades. I have heard the stories of how he beat his wife before his accident." She crosses herself, mumbles, "An act of God, all that machinery that fell on him."

"God?" Consuelo repeats, keeps her gaze on the heap of tamales. Lopsided, uneven. It is suddenly important that things be put into order. She rearranges the stuffed corn husks, says, "But maldades according to what person? One man's criminal is another man's hero. How can we know with what eyes God sees the man? Do you understand?" She looks out the screen, searches for the meaning of her own thoughts as she speaks.

"Ah-huh," Esperanza says, "pues, I don't know about all that. But in Lázaro's case, well, all I got to say is he's not going to rest until his wife and daughter forgive him. Something like that. Things can't be finished for him yet. Problem is, he don't know they don't live here no more, so now the man disturbs *my* sleep. And what business is it of mine? Answer me that, comadre."

"Have the curandera mix you a tea for sleeping," Consuelo says. She stands up with the platter of tamales, turns her back to end the subject, slides the plate into the refrigerator.

"So, when does your son return?" Esperanza says so suddenly, Consuelo starts. "I have never met him, always he's away on trips," Esperanza continues. "Where does he go?"

Consuelo studies Esperanza's face for signs of betrayal. Even though Joaquín tells the details of his trips only to Consuelo and those directly involved, some of the neighbors understand what he is about, but that is precisely why they do not ask too many questions. What a person knows, a person might reveal.

Still, there are times when he has trusted too much. Hasn't she told him repeatedly that you can never know for sure who your enemies are? They can look just like you. Like that woman at the top of the hill. But now in Esperanza's eyes she sees only indifference, or at most, an interest born from the love of gossip.

"Oh, at times he goes away on business," Consuelo says, "other times the university in Tucson—you know he will study there next year." She would like to speak of his achievements, but she'll leave that for others to do. Better not tempt fate, bring down a punishment from God for boasting.

Esperanza looks around Consuelo, through the adjoining door to the framed photograph on the chest of drawers. "Everyone says he is even more good-looking in person," she says, "like an artista de cine, a movie star." She quickly adds, "Not that I am impressed by looks. No, no, look at my Mono, so ugly on the outside, but such a heart. He gives me my pick of all the treasures he finds on his job. Even when this makes his sister very angry, well, she used to get all the best, you know."

Consuelo nods, stretches her lips back into a smile, hears what Esperanza has said, but her thoughts stay with the comment about Joaquín. She has often wondered if some of his tagalongs are more impressed with his handsome face than with his words. Like that mixed-up girl Nancy. Joaquín says she wants to learn of her Mexican

171 Chasing Shadows

heritage because her mother has robbed her of it, but Consuelo met the girl. Nancy followed Joaquín's every movement with warm, damp eyes. No, it was not a sense of history or passion for truth and justice that quickened the pulse in the girl's throat. Better the girl searches for her blood somewhere else. Joaquín must not be distracted from his mission in life.

Esperanza is silent, and Consuelo understands the bride-to-be wants encouragement to turn the conversation back to herself. She asks Esperanza to tell her once again how she and Mono met. She has already heard many times how Esperanza was taking out the trash for her employers when here came the garbage truck with her true love riding the outside floorboard. Still, the story always makes Consuelo smile. Now is a good time to hear of unexpected love. Of love promised eternally. Of the illusion that it is true.

The next morning she arises before the sun, strains her ears for Joaquín's footsteps, but the outside light brings nothing more than the dawn. She tells herself she will not worry about Joaquín today, it will only be bad luck, that if she doesn't think about it, he will come home all the sooner. Didn't Rogelio tell her that yesterday evening when he arrived from work? Now he lies in the bed they have shared for thirty years and pretends to be asleep. She understands he's trying to convince her he is not worried for their baby, and hopes she will believe him; then maybe he can believe his own self-deception.

Mono and Esperanza stroll, hand in hand, beneath the light of tiny colored bulbs strung among the mesquites, mingle with their guests. Esperanza's nervous voice zigzags through the evening air. The twilight has brought a cool breeze, but Mono's face still glistens with perspiration.

Consuelo watches drops of oily sweat pop out of his large pores, gather, then run down the deep creases along each side of his mouth. She has always thought of them as laugh lines, but now, beneath the swaying lights, shadows make his face unreal, a Yaqui mask, expressions etched by rivers of tears.

One of Joaquín's many friends, Mono once told Consuelo, "I like to talk with your son, señora, even though he is only nineteen. When I am with him, he always makes me believe I am more than who I am." She remembers how she was struck by the truth of that comment.

She takes her seat, a kitchen chair propped against the outside wall of her apartment, away from the groups of people dancing, spilling out of the apartment and onto the narrow strip of concrete outside. The windows are open, and the music of Pérez Prado, captured on a black vinyl disk spinning on Joaquín's new record player, blares out from the inside.

She knows the music must still be playing because feet slide across the pavement, hips sway, but she hears only the chirp of the crickets in the surrounding darkness. The party has been going on for three hours now, and Consuelo is glad she has wrapped a bundle of sweet-bean tamales for Joaquín, saved them behind a pitcher of cold water in the refrigerator. When he returns, she will sit with him at the kitchen table, watch his face turn back into that of the little boy who always begged for just one more tamale.

Her eyes roam the lot. Rogelio has left, claims he has unfinished business downtown. She understands that the absence of their son weighs too heavily on him. And no sign of the girl Nancy or her mother. Didn't Consuelo tell Joaquín that it was hopeless to invite them, to try and include them? La Cookie watches over her daughter closely; no way she would allow her to come alone. And Cookie is

173

not ready to join them. Consuelo looks up the hill, thinks of the binoculars that she saw reflected only yesterday. Didn't Consuelo warn him it is dangerous to force people to face a truth they cannot accept?

Her gaze now returns to her guests, focuses, narrows to the mouths opening, shutting. Fish, waiting to be fed. She is reminded of something her mother used to tell her. Cover your mouth when you yawn, she would say, otherwise evil spirits can get in. Consuelo wonders why they must be evil, why not any spirit? She wants to open her mouth wider than she ever has, to scream until no sound comes out, stretch her lips even more, a cave.

Her eyes burn. She didn't think she had any tears left in her. She eases out of her chair. No one notices as she presses back inside the apartment, across the kitchen, pushes open the closed door to her bedroom, squeezes in quietly. From the outside, light filters through the curtains, allows her to make her way to the chest of drawers, pick up the framed photograph of Joaquín. Old eyes, always he had old eyes.

Even when he was a small boy, she remembers thinking that he already saw things she couldn't see. So many things left undone. If something happens to him, what happens to the dream?

From outside, she hears Esperanza's voice, scratching at the window screen. Still complaining of Lázaro, of his soul that can't rest.

A knock on her bedroom door. Consuelo looks up, stares, but does not move.

"Soy yo," a small voice says.

For a fractioned second, the boy's voice is her son's ten years ago. Borders blur, past and present blending in her mind. He repeats, "Soy yo, Flaco."

She watches the doorknob, the cautious twist before the door edges open. When he does appear, she realizes that the loud laughter outside has stopped. Whispers, like small ghosts, *shush-shushing* at her bedroom wall, waiting to get in.

"Señora?" Flaco whispers. "You here? Look, Doña Pilar says to bring you food. She says you ain't ate nothing all night."

Consuelo switches on the lamp, motions for the boy to put the small lidded saucepan on the end table.

He sets it on a doily, taps a finger on the lid. "Soup made from the rooster," he says. "Doña Pilar says it will give you courage to endure. Them's her words, exact," he says.

He bites at the skin on his thumb, lifts his gaze. She holds it and they share a thought. His eyes go red before he looks to the side. Consuelo presses her palm against the picture frame. If only she could draw him back inside her, his spirit in the safety of her womb. Flaco places his hand on hers. When she closes her eyes, it is as though—for just a moment—all the dreams she passed on to Joaquín return, pulse back into her heart.